I SHALL SURVIVE USING POTIONS!

6

Author: FUNA
Illustrator: Sukima

I Shall Survive Using Potions! Volume 6
by FUNA

Translated by Hiroya Watanabe
Edited by William Haggard
English Cover & Lettering by Kelsey Denton

Copyright © 2020 FUNA
Illustrations by Sukima

First published in Japan in 2020 by Kodansha Ltd., Tokyo.
Publication rights for this English edition arranged through Kodansha Ltd., Tokyo.

Find more books like this one at www.j-novel.club!

Managing Director: Samuel Pinansky
Light Novel Line Manager: Chi Tran
Managing Editor: Jan Mitsuko Cash
Managing Translator: Kristi Fernandez
QA Manager: Hannah N. Carter
Marketing Manager: Stephanie Hii

ISBN: 978-1-7183-7195-8
Printed in Korea
First Printing: October 2021
10 9 8 7 6 5 4 3 2 1

CONTENTS

I SHALL SURVIVE USING POTIONS

Design
Hyakuashiya Yuuko + Tanigome Kabuto
(musicagographics)

Chapter 42:
Status Check

There I was, in His Majesty the King's office, which was smack-dab in the middle of the royal palace, having forgotten that I had sworn to the Goddess that I would never again set foot in here. I have to provide a logical explanation for this...

"It's been a while, Your Majesty. I know I made a solemn vow that I'd never come back here, but I'm sure glad I made sure to ask Celes for an exception for emergencies and other important situations!"

There, problem solved!

"Ah... Right..."

It seemed the king was a bit embarrassed about crying to his older brother in front of others, and his face was slightly red.

Roland treated the king with indifference, but I didn't have anything against the guy. He was the king of this country, after all, so I was going to interact with him accordingly. I mean, I didn't want any rumors going around that the Angel had more authority than His Majesty the King.

...I had already given up on claiming I wasn't the Angel long ago.

AHHH~

"So, what's the situation in the Kingdom of Brancott?" Roland asked as he pushed the king back, given how he was clinging onto him, with no small amount of annoyance on Roland's part.

"Yes, let me explain. Please take a seat," the king said, gesturing toward a sofa for guests and sitting down himself.

As his guests, we weren't allowed to sit down before he did. That is, unless we were kings from other countries ourselves. But if we had actually been foreign monarchs, we wouldn't have been greeted in a room like this.

A maid brought us some drinks, then the others were dismissed, leaving just our party and the king.

Once everyone else left, Roland's younger brother Serge — the king — explained the details to us. According to him, it was all just as we had been told by the royal guard. The king of the neighboring kingdom of Brancott had suddenly passed away, causing an all-too-familiar contest for succession. Normally, it would have gone to that annoying first prince Fernand, but the second in line, Ghislain, was also vying for the throne.

They were both children of the princess consort, so there weren't any issues like the first prince's mother being of a lower class while the second prince's mother was the daughter of a marquis or anything like that, but instead it seemed like the selfish and greedy second son just wanted to take the throne and supplant the hard-working and honest first son. I had only ever seen Fernand as a stalker who caused me problems, but he was actually fairly respectable about things that didn't involve me. That was pretty surprising...

So anyway, there was no official successor appointed because of the previous king's sudden passing... Well, there wasn't really a need for one, because everyone assumed the first prince would take over...

11

But some folks decided to use that as part of their plot to appoint the second prince instead.

Their reasoning went like this: "The first prince has displeased the Angel, so if he becomes king, we'll lose the protection of the Goddess and our kingdom will crumble." Some idiot had made up that rumor and started spreading it around.

Not to mention, there were self-proclaimed high priests in the royal palace, in an entirely separate hierarchy from the priests of the Temple of the Goddess. They'd been making connections through bribery and had joined the second prince's faction, hoping to put the easily-manipulated boy on the throne for their own benefit.

The Temple of the Goddess hadn't accepted these shady newcomers, but stayed silent because they couldn't deny that the first prince had displeased the Angel...

Then there was the previous king's demise. Word was that he had seemed healthy but had then suddenly died of an illness, which could mean he'd been poisoned...

The first prince should have been the crown prince in the first place, and considering the fact that he was more suitable and better-liked than his younger brother, the succession should have been a smooth process. And yet, the second prince's faction had started firing off unsubstantiated claims that the late king had appointed the second prince as his successor, then launched a sudden attack on the first prince's faction — which denied their claim, of course — and took the royal palace by force.

Fortunately for them, the first prince and his confidants had managed to flee by using a hidden escape route that was only known to the royal heir, and he's been missing ever since.

"A pretty common story..." I said.

"Indeed," Roland agreed.

"Meanwhile, there are brothers who try to push the duty of being king onto each other because they'd rather not deal with it..." I noted.

"Hahaha..." the king replied, shoulders drooping at my words as he chuckled listlessly.

Welp, you never know what'll happen! Gotta keep your chin up!

"So, the second prince, Ghislain, is currently in control of the royal palace, but it seems no one believes he is the legitimate heir, not even those who are trying to put him on the throne. Everyone is either staying silent out of fear of being purged then and there, or are otherwise trying to benefit from backing the winning horse. They will surely crumble as soon as the tides turn. Therefore..."

"They want to take out their greatest threat, which is you, the first prince..." I replied.

"Indeed. If that happens, the line of succession would technically devolve onto the second prince. Though, whether a usurper who murders his father and older brother has the right to succeed the throne is another matter altogether..."

Of course, someone like that had absolutely no right to become a ruler. Even if the first prince was out of the picture, someone else of royal blood should take over instead. The late king had a daughter, and his younger brother had children too. It wasn't as if there were no successors left if the second prince was to be disinherited. And it wasn't as if the second prince could just massacre all of the other successors, their collateral lines, and everyone else related to the royal family.

Then Serge began to fill us in on the response status of his own country.

"I've dispatched the Four Walls to the eastern border. I determined that the Kingdom of Aseed to the south and the Aligot

Empire to the west were less of a threat, so the arrangements there are the same as usual. Though, that said, I haven't extracted any soldiers from those regions, just in case.

"The remaining forces of the standing army and the conscripts have been sent to the eastern border as well. The Kingdom of Aseed has also gathered their forces along the border they share with the Kingdom of Brancott as well as on the side closest to us. They've agreed to cross the border and send us reinforcements as soon as we request it."

"Perfect. We can't make the first move, so all that's left now is to wait for them to declare war or cross our border without warning."

"Yes. We will be intercepting the enemy's attack, so the battle will take place on our territory. It's a shame that our land will be ruined as a result, but there's nothing we can do about that..."

It seemed that he had taken care of what needed to be done, despite his initial lack of self-confidence. Though, really, I didn't think Roland would have left him to be king if he was completely incompetent. I sympathized with him, considering that he was always being compared to Roland, but he probably would have been a fine king even if Roland had never been in the picture.

"There's no such thing as a younger brother who's better than his older brother!" as someone used to say...

Anyway, the Kingdom of Balmore couldn't take any action until Brancott did something first, so they had to cede the initiative out of necessity. They couldn't be the ones to spark the war, but Serge was right that they had to take on the giant disadvantage of the battle taking place on their home turf. They didn't really have a choice in the matter, considering that the Kingdom of Balmore had their position and reputation to consider.

...But none of that had anything to do with me. The enemy had used my name for personal gain, put words in my mouth, and attacked Layette and me. It was an undeniable fact that they had already declared war on me. In fact, you could even say they had launched a surprise attack on me *without* a declaration of war. So I had the right to strike back, right? Me personally, I mean.

"Okay, we'll be going now!"

"Huh?" Roland, Francette, and the king all said, looking at me with wide eyes.

"I mean, we just came here to drop off Roland. We did what we came here to do, so we're leaving. Is that an issue?"

"Whaaaaaat?!"

What, did they think I was gonna help them with their war?

"I have no intention of favoring one side of a mortal war over another."

"…" Roland and the king were stunned into silence and looked at me as if they hadn't expected this at all.

Francette was surprised at first when I announced I was leaving, but didn't seem too caught off-guard when I explained I didn't intend to help in their war. Emile, Belle, and Layette were as cool as cucumbers, of course. It seemed that Roland was the only one who didn't understand me at all.

After all this time we had spent together… And he was supposed to be the smartest one here, too… It just went to show that smarts and the ability to understand people weren't one and the same.

And so, I left the rather conflicted-looking Roland and the king behind and headed back to the residence of the Eyes of the Goddess.

…Indeed, I wasn't going to provide any help for their war. This was *my* war, after all. I'm not helping *them* because *I'm* the real combatant here. I'll be the one attacking Brancott, not the other way around.

That was fine and all, but… Why was Francette following me instead of staying behind? And with such a happy smile, too…?

"I'm home!"

Thud thud thud thud thud thud! came the sound of feet down the stairs, as several voices all piped up in unison.

"Welcome home!!!"

I had returned home for the first time in several months. Though, really, this place felt like it actually belonged to the orphans and I was just staying over... But it wasn't as if I was just lying around and slacking off. I simply tasked the orphans with cooking, cleaning, laundry, making a living, and everything else to cultivate their independence! That was why they were able to live on their own without me or Emile there.

Not only had I taught the girls how to do housework, but I'd also instructed the boys, too. I wasn't so anachronistic that I'd only taught the boys how to go out and hold down a job while teaching the girls to do housework! Though I guess that was actually considered a standard practice rather than an anachronism in this world...

That said, I had been sure to teach them to take care of themselves without depending on others, regardless of their gender. I wanted to make sure they could support themselves on their own before they found marriage partners, and I didn't want them to end up being scumbags who dumped all of the housework and childcare on their wives after getting married. As a result, they all ended up being fine young kids. Each of them grew up to be capable of doing housework for me.

I'm the one who raised them!

I had already let them know about my return with the sound resonance crystal set, so while they were happy about my return, they weren't all that surprised. If I had suddenly come home without giving them a heads-up, they might have wet themselves like overly excited puppies. No, seriously.

I wasn't gonna have them report to me on what I had missed in my absence. I'd been keeping in touch and getting info in real time with the crystal set, after all. Even though I had told them many times that they didn't need to report so frequently, the kids were so eager to talk to me that they took every opportunity they could to chat about whatever.

Telling me that onions were a copper coin cheaper at the vegetable shop in Brancott's royal capital wasn't really useful information...

Anyway, I was back home for the first time in a while. I decided to lie on the ground and have the kids step on my back. It actually felt really good...

"Gueh!"

I just made a weird noise. Wait…

"Quit it! You're crushing me! Belle, you're way past stepping on my back already! Anyone who gets too heavy gets relieved of stepping-on-my-back duty. Off you go!"

Belle stepped off of my back, looking a little sad. I really couldn't compromise on this, even though she was making those puppy-dog eyes. If I left her to it, she'd snap my spine in two.

As Belle moved away, an older but smaller child moved in on the now-vacant spot on my back.

That's right, Belle, blame your own body for growing so much… Especially your boobs! That's why you lost the privilege of stepping on my back!

"Gagh! D-Don't jump on me! And not three of you at once!!!"

My insides were about to burst out of my mouth!

And so, I spent my time being a degenerate for a while…

Come to think of it, even if I was gonna deal with the enemy, it was better to have them cross the border, both in consideration of this country's situation and in terms of dishing out divine punishment.

Picking a fight with the Angel was reason enough to get back at them, but if they invaded the country where the Angel lived, that would make them seem all the more villainous. Plus, if they crossed the border and fulfilled the conditions to activate the secret alliance with the Kingdom of Aseed, it would make things more convenient in the long term.

And so, I had Francette take care of gathering information from the king and focused on spending time with the children (leaving all the work for others to do and basically lazing about)…

Oh, and I introduced Layette to everyone as a new member of the Eyes of the Goddess.

She was with us all this time, but a girl her age should have been living with the other kids here. Such a young child being among all these adults by herself wasn't a good environment for her. Not to mention, we were about to head into battle…

I couldn't bring her with us. So, I had to have Layette live here with the others as a member of the Eyes of the Goddess. I was going to miss having her around for emotional support, but I couldn't drag her around for my own selfish reasons. I had to endure! I could come back to see her any time…

Then I educated the children on various topics before bedtime. The thing is, they were all good, honest kids who revered me as a goddess, but…they were a bit too dependent on me. They should be able to stand on their own without me, but not one of them wanted to leave.

The oldest of them, Emile, was currently sixteen and would be seventeen soon. The youngest one, excluding Layette, was Belle at twelve years old. I mean, they were all old enough to find work as live-in apprentices, craftsmen-in-training, hunters, or military cadets.

In other words, they were at the age to be considered normal members of society who had lost their parents at a young age, and a few of them, like Emile, were already of age. They weren't just orphans anymore. An ex-orphan with no guarantor or connections would normally have had a hard time getting hired anywhere, but no employer would turn down someone who had lived with me and been taken under my wing. If they tried, they could have gotten hired at any major business they wanted. Maybe they could have even found work as servants in a noble household.

…So why hadn't they gone out into the world already?! In the four years before I left on my journey, I taught them so much during our before-bedtime discussions! Cooking, reading, writing, math, the workings of society, how to make money, and common scams — not to scam others, but to avoid falling for them, of course. Plus, some basic chemistry, physics, medical science, and more...

I even told them all sorts of stories so they wouldn't get bored. Mainly stories from Japanese manga and anime, along with some mythology and folktales from Earth... They probably thought these were true stories from my world at first, but they had to know they were make-believe stories by now.

Anyway, I gave them enough training to get hired at most places. So why had none of them tried to leave this orphanage?! I get that it was easier to save money because they didn't have to pay rent and food was cheap here, but they couldn't live together forever. They would all eventually have to find a lover or get married.

...Wait, Emile and Belle better not get all lovey-dovey in front of everyone here! That may be fine by society's standards, but not mine! Such insolence wasn't gonna fly in my book!

Haah... Haah...

In any case, I had given them this house, so if they wanted to live here until they got married to cut down on living expenses, that was totally fine.

But why did they insist on working at places where they could commute from here? Even if they had to find live-in work or go someplace far away, they had to consider their future... Why couldn't they just think of this place as a home they could return to? There was no reason to stay here all the time. Or maybe this home that I bestowed on them was more like a curse binding them here...

"Hey, why don't you kids try to find proper careers with future prospects instead of working as messenger boys, store clerks, or nursemaids? I know you're all capable of..."

"You're the one that taught us that all occupations are equally honorable, Kaoru!"

"Urgh…"

"There's lots of baggage that comes with regular employment, like excessive responsibilities that are disproportionate to the salary, human relations, and expectations of unpaid work or work on holidays. And women have to deal with harassment from superiors who abuse their positions of power…"

"Urggh…"

Damn, they sound just like permanent part-time employees… And I'm the one who taught them all this… This was bad. Really bad.

"Don't you guys want to become independent soon? I don't intend on living here forever, so I was thinking of moving on… And if you all move out, I could sell this place and divvy up the money to help you all on your fresh new starts."

Yes, if I could just sell this place off, they would all fly freely off into the world. And once this current incident was resolved, I planned to go on another journey right away. I did plan on staying a legal resident of this country, for the record. I was just going on a journey, and as long as I was considered an inhabitant of this city, it would make it easier for me and avoid all sorts of trouble later on.

If I wandered around on my journey without being registered anywhere and people found out who I was, they would probably get pushy about having me live in their country. Plus, I'd feel bad if this country became known for being abandoned by the Angel. So I would continue living here in a formal, legal capacity, but that didn't mean I had to leave this house here if no one was living in it. And the kids would end up being stuck in this house if I did just leave it here, which would be a huge waste of talent.

If these kids went out into the world and put all their knowledge and education they had gotten here to good use, it would make this country — no, the world — a better place. Maybe just a little bit…

It would also lead to their own happiness, and I would have a small part in doing something good for this world, which would make me kind of happy too.

Wait…they seem pretty shaken by what I had said…

"D-D-Do you mean…"

"Are you going back to the heavenly realm, Big Sis Kaoru…?"

"Y-You're leaving us?"

Oh no, they're about to burst into tears! …Actually, some of them are crying already!

But I couldn't just baby them here. I had to give it to them straight, here and now.

"I can't just live with all of you here forever. I…"

"Wh-Wh-What is it?"

They were on the verge of tears, but I declared without mercy: "I'll get married and live a life of my own someday…"

"Oh, we'll be fine for a while, then!"

…What was with their relieved smiles?! How incredibly rude…

"Oh, but I need to manage my own world too! Just like Celes…"

Indeed, I was generally known as a friend of the Goddess Celestine… Most people continued to call me the Angel, no matter how desperately I denied it, though. And so, I was supposed to be a normal human girl who was loved by the Goddess, but some people, like these kids, Francette, Roland, House Adan, and a few others, thought of me as a goddess of another world. So this explanation was fine for them.

"That's why I need to leave soon…"

"…"

The children went silent. It seemed like they wanted to stop me but considered that I may have important work as a goddess, or maybe they were worried that the citizens of my world were in trouble without me.

They looked like they were about to cry again, but they seemed to understand they couldn't be selfish here and said nothing. And I understood I had to be firm here. If I coddled them out of sympathy, nothing would change. I had to keep my emotions out of this…

"Do you think people who try to keep the Goddess for themselves and rely on her without trying to live by their own abilities deserve the Goddess's blessing?"

I ignored the sobs as I turned my back and walked toward my room.

…I was the one who wanted to cry!

"…"

I woke up the next day and went into the living room to find the kids hanging their heads at the dining table. They all had red eyes. And yet they had prepared breakfast, including mine, of course.

I sat down and thanked them for breakfast, then they mumbled listlessly in response...

"Sheesh, who died?! Get a grip! Remember what I taught you all? Be cheerful during mealtimes! Even if you're sad or in pain, be energetic and happy when you eat, even if you have to fake it! Otherwise, you'll just make the food taste bad and feel even worse!"

Usually, the kids at least forced themselves to smile when I gave a pep talk like this, but they all still looked like the world was ending.

"B-But..."

"I just can't..."

"Urgh... Waaah..."

This was hopeless... I had to do something or they were gonna end up as empty husks...

"Do you think someone who doesn't try to live by their own abilities deserves my blessing?"

"But if we do become capable of living on our own, you'll leave us..."

That was a good point... I had already left once, but maybe they thought I was going on a journey to find a husband, and I was going to come back once I did. They had said they would continue to protect this house and wait for me, and Emile and Belle had left with me. Maybe they were afraid I could leave for good next time.

Hmm... There wasn't really anything I could do here...

Chapter 43:
The Battle Begins

Three days have passed.

During that time, I went to make excuses to Achille's older brother's wife. I told him that I wasn't lying around and making the children do all the work because I was lazy, but I was doing so intentionally to foster their ability to take care of themselves and be self-reliant…

She asked me if I was telling the truth, so I told her to look into my eyes. She stared at my face…and then said, "You're lying!"

How did she know?!

Anyway, I made up an excuse and got outta there! Next, I went to visit Maillart Workshop.

Of course, I saw my replacement Lolotte every day (come to think of it, why was she at the house every day even though she's supposed to be living and working at the workshop?), but I had to find out what was up with Achille's whole "inviting Lolotte to be his lover" thing. So I marched over there, and Achille suddenly prostrated himself in a gesture of total submission.

...Did he think I was gonna kill him or something? Was it because of my scary eyes? Hey, shaddap!

Well, I suppose things were different when he was just the third son of a viscount, but it would be difficult to take in an orphan as his lawful wife now that he was a big-shot baron. It would have been one thing if Lolotte could have been a concubine whose child would be born as an aristocrat, but if she was going to be a throwaway lover with no rights, and if her child would end up with no claim to their inheritance or any status as an aristocrat, it would be pretty rough for her despite having married into a wealthy family...

It was possible for her to become a foster daughter of a noble family just for form's sake, but there weren't a lot of aristocrats who would take in a commoner orphan, even if temporarily and only on paper. Unless they were really desperate for money and offered a big payout in return, that is...

I mean, they would probably accept with reluctance if I personally requested it. But I didn't think it was quite right to force someone to do something they didn't want to, especially if it could affect their house's reputation.

No, I knew there was a way. I could accept the title Roland had prepared for me and adopt Lolotte myself. I wouldn't have minded having her as a step-daughter at all, and no aristocrat would turn down my daughter, adopted or not, to take in as their lawful wife.

It was the perfect plan... That is, if you ignore two issues with that.

First, I had no intention of becoming an aristocrat. I didn't want any unnecessary duties or burdens on my shoulders, and I definitely wasn't cool with being bound to this country.

The other issue was that this would be far too much favoritism. The Eyes of the Goddess had met me at an early stage, and they received preferential treatment from me compared to all the other orphans. There were so many orphans in the royal capital...no, in this entire country. It wasn't like I could help all of them. I had met them by chance and they had just happened to help me out, so I took care of them for a bit to repay them. Arranging for one of them to become the lawful wife of an aristocrat was way too much.

Lolotte needed to get through this on her own and make her own life decisions using the hand she was dealt. It wasn't for me to butt in. So...

"...Well, good luck!"

With that, I patted Achille on the shoulder, said my greetings to Bardot, the owner of the workshop, as well as the others, then left after having a little chat.

After some time, Francette returned from the royal palace with some intel.

"It seems the Brancott army has begun mobilizing. There are many aristocrats and military commanders who oppose this move, but they couldn't refuse orders from their king and superiors out of fear for their jobs and lives..."

No surprise there. They'd be lucky if the punishment had just stopped there, but their whole family could have ended up getting slaughtered if they didn't do as they were told.

The first prince wouldn't have done anything so stupid himself, but the second prince knew he wasn't as well-liked as him and had taken the throne by force. But if he knew the first prince was still alive, he'd surely be desperate to crush his opposition with all his available force...

And even though this would just result in him losing even more popularity, those who were putting him up on a pedestal weren't doing anything to stop him.

Not surprising, really. It was convenient for them if the prince took out the people in his way, and they'd only put a target on their own backs if they tried to stop him. If they truly were just in it for their own profit rather than for the country or its people, there was no way they would put themselves in danger for no reason.

"When will they arrive at the border?"

"In four days. They will likely be close to it on the evening of the third day. They should camp the night there, then cross the border in the morning."

Yeah, it wouldn't make sense to enter enemy territory in the evening and camp overnight there.

"Then let's get there by the morning of the third day, just in case. We should depart tomorrow morning, I think."

There were all sorts of factors at play, like the time it would take for their spies to report, but it takes time, logistically speaking, to move fully equipped armies. I had nothing to carry, thanks to the Item Box, and they couldn't possibly compete with Ed's potion-augmented speed, so I'd have plenty of time to get there.

"What about the royal army?"

"They were already prepared to mobilize, so they're ready to go at any time. Of course, there were some troops who had already been deployed, so once the army regroups with them, the combined force will likely engage the enemy about a day's march away from the border. That area is a barren wasteland, with no residents nearby, so it's an ideal battlefield."

Yeah, no one was stupid enough to start a fight in a granary. Oh, but I guess it wouldn't matter if it belonged to an enemy, unless victory was guaranteed, and you knew you were going to claim that territory afterward.

"Okay then, time to sleep for the big day tomorrow!"

"…"

Ah, the kids were listening from behind me and looked pretty concerned…

"Why do you look so worried? Do you think mere mortals can do anything to me?"

"…"

Well, I suppose they couldn't help but worry, even if I was a so-called goddess. So…

"Don't worry, on the off-chance that something does happen to me, this body is only temporary. Even if it gets destroyed, it won't have any effect on me. Worst-case scenario, this little vacation of mine will end a bit quicker than planned, and I'd just go back to my own world. I probably have a lot of work waiting for me…"

Oh no, it had the opposite effect! They got even gloomier… On the other hand, Francette and Emile look pretty pleased! Francette is one thing, but I'm not taking you, Emile!

"Whaaaaaat?!" Emile and Belle screamed in shock when I told them I wasn't bringing them with me.

Of course I'm not! Emile may be a hard worker, but his skill level is only somewhere between that of a common foot soldier and a veteran soldier. He wasn't strong enough to guarantee his survival on the battlefield. As for Belle, she wouldn't even qualify as a disposable sacrificial shield.

I mean, there's no such thing as guaranteed survival no matter how strong someone is. You could always get struck by a stray arrow, surrounded by enemies, or who knows what else. Even Francette had suffered a fatal wound in the war against the Aligot Empire four and a half years ago... This time, of course, we weren't going to fight like we had back then.

But I had to appease them somehow, or they would insist on tagging along...

All right!

"Why would I want to waste my most reliable trump cards on a chaotic battlefield? I want you guys to protect everyone here and prepare for the worst. In other words, stay on standby here and prepare to protect me during the last stand for the royal capital."

"Yes!" Belle and Emile replied enthusiastically.

...They were so easy.

The day before the Brancott army was expected to cross the border, we calculated the distance the invaders would travel from the border in a day (including their support troops), anticipated that the Balmore royal army would be deployed in the wasteland there, and moved even farther ahead. ...Basically, we snuck around without greeting the royal army.

I hadn't brought the children with us, of course, and the king was back at the palace instead of at the front lines.

Roland was a bit farther behind us and leading the main forces. It was probably a veteran general giving out the actual directions, so he was more of a figurehead.

So it was just me here, along with...

"Why are you here, Francette...? You're supposed to be Roland's guard!"

"What? But you granted me the title of Einherjar, the Guardian of the Goddess, that one time."

"Urgh!"

…I had just been going with the flow then, but I *did* remember saying something like that.

"B-But you're a noble and a knight, and it's your duty as Roland's guard to…"

"I am a liaison officer."

"Huh?"

"A liaison officer."

"Whaaat?"

"A liaison officer."

"Whaaaaaa!"

…Damn! Oh well.

Unlike Emile, Francette was an upstanding adult, even from my point of view as Kaoru Nagase the Japanese woman rather than the Kaoru of this world. She was around thirty, and had lived much longer than me, too… As such, she could make and take responsibility for her own decisions. Yes, Francette didn't need me doing this and that to protect her. She should be the one protecting me.

And so, the number of forces charging into the middle of the Brancott army came to a grand total of two people.

What about us?

Oh, my mistake. Two people and two horses — Ed, and Francette's beloved horse.

All right then, time to rock!

"But let's have some tea for now."

"Yes!"

We had arrived early, just in case, but the enemy wasn't expected to arrive until tomorrow afternoon. And so, we decided to pull out a tent, beds, chairs, a table, and a tea set, and wait for them to show up.

Some time past noon the next day...

The Brancott army could be seen in the distance. Of course, both the Brancott and Balmore armies had sent out preliminary troops to scout ahead, so each of the factions must have known each other's positions.

We quickly packed up the tent. Surely they would completely ignore two young girls and their horses just standing there without giving them so much as a second glance. They wouldn't bother trying anything with a harmless lookout or two at this point.

And so, we watched as the two armies closed in on each other and waited for the right timing.

The Balmore army waited for the enemy as the Brancott army moved in, closing the distance between them to about 700 to 800 meters, which meant there was still plenty of time before they started firing their bows at each other. I hopped onto Ed and charged in between the two armies from the side. Then...

Boooooooom!!!

The "nitroglycerin-like substance" made a huge explosion up in the sky. Yup, it was that same, familiar stuff I used before. It came in a gourd-shaped container and spawned with two types of chemicals that would mix and cause an explosion right away.

The entire Brancott army froze immediately. Now was the time to bust out the loudspeaker-type potion container.

"To the usurper's rebel army, which plots to invade the country that the Goddess Celestine has bestowed upon her friend, I say this: you shall fall straight to hell!"

Boom! Bam! Bang!

Glass balls containing something like nitroglycerin rained down from the sky and exploded one after another. They each landed a bit in front of the Brancott army, but weren't causing any damage. Physical damage, that is.

"Wh-Whaaat?! But they told me the Angel abandoned Balmore! I thought the Kingdom of Balmore was no longer loved by the Goddess!"

"I was told the Angel supports Lord Ghislain's claim to the throne! They said this is a holy war and the Goddess is with us! So why is the Angel on their side and we're treated as the rebel blasphemers?! That's not what I heard at all!"

"They tricked us! We were lied to by those usurping, blasphemous bastards! I don't wanna go to hell! I don't want my family to get struck down by the Goddess!"

"Hell no! I didn't become a soldier just to get killed as an enemy of the Goddess and go to hell! I just wanted to fight for my family, for my country, for justice! I just wanted to protect everyone's happiness!!!"

It was complete chaos. Some men cried and screamed as they clung to their commanders, others tried to retreat, while others threw their weapons to the ground... No one was concerned with fighting a war against Balmore anymore.

There wasn't a single life, weapon, or resource lost. And yet, the Brancott army was wiped out psychologically before the battle even began.

"Open the way."

Fwssh!

I gave the order through the loudspeaker-type potion container, then the sea of people parted, opening a straight path through.

...Who am I, Moses?!

Anyway, the soldiers all fell to their knees, and I walked through the newly-created path with Francette, who was all smiles. Oh, and we were both riding our horses, of course. But man, Francette sure seemed thrilled whenever I did Goddess-like stuff...

In any case, we kept moving forward. With that done, the soldiers should turn back and retreat from here. It was a good thing the battle had ended without any needless casualties on either side. The soldiers were simply following orders, but it wasn't as if they had strongly believed in their cause this time.

If they understood everything that was going on and were still dead-set on killing the enemy and seizing their riches for their own country, without any intention of listening to the other side, I would have had no choice but to give them a harsh reality check. But if they knew who I was and could be convinced through a simple explanation, that was fine by me.

"Destination: Aras, the royal capital of the Kingdom of Brancott. Let's go!"

"Yeah!"

"Breeehehehe!"

I glanced behind me and saw the Balmore frontline soldiers just standing there, having done absolutely nothing...

Yeah, I was glad I couldn't really see their expressions because they were somewhat far away.

My bad!

"Lady Kaoru, what shall we do next?"

Now that she was back in her own country and I was acting as a goddess, Francette was back to addressing me as "Lady Kaoru." Oh well.

"We should be able to head straight to the capital with the method we just used. I'm sure the Balmore army and Brancott army will follow too... And if we move forward normally without rushing too much, post horses should deliver their reports before we get there.

"The first prince, who should be hiding somewhere and keeping an eye on the situation; the men of his faction who had no choice

35

but to reluctantly follow the second prince's orders; and the original priests of the Temple of the Goddess in Brancott...they should all have heard about what just happened by the time we get there...

"So, we'll be marching right in through the front door after giving the other forces enough time to gather, march in, and join us."

Francette grinned, but then she looked a little worried as she brought up a question.

"Um, Lady Kaoru. I will have a chance to be of use to you, won't I?"

...Not my problem!

"What? Kaoru has returned to Balmore?! And she's leading the Balmore army and our own invading troops to strike down the blasphemer Ghislain?! Ahh! The Goddess's blessing is with us! Contact any aristocrats and dignitaries who will answer our call at once! And only those with a trust ranking of A. Don't contact B-ranks or lower until the very last moment to avoid the information getting leaked!

"As for the Temple of the Goddess, contact only the archbishop. Emphasize to him that the other priests are only to be contacted after the uprising takes place."

"Yes, my lord!" Fernand's confidants moved out at his orders.

"So, Kaoru is here. Hmhm... Hahaha..."

"You shouldn't get too optimistic... The counterattack is one thing, but afterward, she isn't..." Fabio warned the grinning first prince Fernand.

"That's right. Kaoru is working for the Kingdoms of Balmore and Brancott, and for their people. She absolutely isn't doing it out of love for you or anything. If you get the wrong idea and get ahead of yourself, it'll end up in disaster. You understand that, don't you?"

"Urgh…" After even being told off by Allan, who had failed in his search for Kaoru but still enjoyed his little trip anyway, Fernand couldn't help but hang his head.

"What?! The Angel is leading the army to the royal capital?! Ah! The forces of the Goddess are with us! Lady Celestine has sent her servant to save our Kingdom of Brancott from the heretics leading her to ruin! Very well, I will keep this a secret for the time being. Once the time comes, we of the Temple of the Goddess will give our lives for the Goddess, the Angel, and the people…"

"Impossible! You're the ones who told me that the Goddess Celestine had forsaken Balmore! You said that Lady Kaoru, the Angel herself, had left the kingdom and was to ally with me to oppose Fernand! So why…?" Ghislain accused the priests, but they had also been taken completely by surprise.

It seemed they weren't too frequently in contact with Bishop Bruce, given that they hadn't been alarmed when they stopped hearing from him. It was also evident that they were not yet aware that Bruce had tried and failed to kill Kaoru, and had been executed after revealing everything he knew.

But as bishops, using eloquence to wheedle their way out of situations was part of their job description.

"I have no idea what you are talking about, my lord… The Angel is leading the army of Balmore to come to beg for your forgiveness! Now that the Kingdom of Balmore's own army has defected to us, along with the Angel, there is no need to ruin the land or slaughter the people, all of whom are about to belong to our kingdom. We only need to demand their complete and total surrender."

"What...?" It was obviously a lie, but a drowning man will clutch even at a straw. Amidst the fear and despair, the second prince Ghislain wanted to — no, had no choice but to — cling to the answer that he wanted most.

"I...I see! So that's it! Damn that messenger for coming back with a false report! Haha, hahaha... Hey, someone behead that messenger from earlier!"

When the crimes of the bishops from the old Holy Land of Rueda had been exposed and their assets were seized, some of them had quickly converted their funds into gold and jewelry, then escaped the country to live the rest of their lives in comfort, while the other bishops rejected their methods and instead plotted their return to power.

Out of those bishops, there was a group who had vowed to get revenge by making their way into the center of the Kingdom of Brancott, a neighbor to the Kingdom of Balmore, which the old Holy Land of Rueda had been absorbed into. They concealed the fact that they had escaped from Rueda and claimed to be bishops on missionary work from a faraway land, so as to curry favor with the second prince. The vast riches they had brought from the Holy Land of Rueda certainly hadn't hurt at all.

The bishops of Brancott considered the first prince to be the clear heir to the throne, making them enemies in the eyes of the dumb second prince who wished to be king. To him, the whispers from the traveling bishops, telling him he was fit to be king and assuring him that it was the will of both the Goddess and the Angel, were quite comfortable to hear, so he ignored the unspoken agreement to keep the church and politics separate. Instead, he kept them close by.

Once convinced, he began spreading their whispers around, in full agreement with what the bishops had said. The second prince claimed that he had just so happened to be the only one near the king at the time of his sudden passing, and that the king's last words were to have Ghislain take the throne in his stead. He then took immediate action to arrest the other would-be king.

But rather than be captured, the first prince used a secret passageway that had been passed down through the kings and the crown princes of each generation, and thus managed to escape with his trusted confidants. The second prince knew that those around him only cared about their own benefit over that of their country, and that there was no telling how his currently-obedient retainers would act if the first prince showed up, so he had no choice but to eliminate his rival and make them accept him as the rightful heir.

In order to pull this off, he initiated a plan to invade the neighboring kingdom of Balmore, effectively killing three birds with one stone by searching for the first prince, getting the military and merchants on his side, and diverting the people from their discontent all at the same time. But, of course, this decision was greatly influenced by the "traveling bishops," who had given him such good advice while relaying "the will of the Goddess." And, of course, her will was for him to unite the Kingdom of Balmore under his rule…

The traveling bishops had one wish: to take over the Kingdom of Balmore, and thus retake Rueda, all while getting revenge against those who had betrayed and banished them! With that done, they would regain all their glory from those days long gone!

…But instead, it was all ending here. They had never expected the Angel to return to the Kingdom of Balmore and launch a full counterattack. Considering that they had raised their soldiers' morale in the face of an invasion on a friendly nation of many years by using the names of the Goddess and the Angel, this turn of events had effectively nullified their military power.

They considered their options, and...

"We must escape! We pulled it off once before, and we just need to do it again. Most of the fortune taken from Rueda is still there. We only need to load it all into the carriage and flee to the center of the continent, then start over again... Only..."

"Yes, we must crush that demon and get our revenge. Once she's gone, the Goddess Celestine will go back to staying out of human affairs for the most part, apart from occasionally warning us of danger..."

The self-proclaimed "traveling bishops," who were actually Rueda's former bishops, were quite optimistic in their views. It was true that the Goddess Celestine hadn't directly punished the bishops from the Holy Land of Rueda, instead only speaking of past events. She had actually left without really doing anything, other than scolding the Pope a bit for misusing the sacred treasure. Depending on how one looked at it, it could be interpreted as refraining from unnecessary interference and thus staying out of human affairs.

It was all because of that damned girl, the one who happened to have the Goddess Celestine's favor. She was the one who forced her interpretation on everyone after the Goddess had left. In their minds, the fall of Rueda was all because of that girl's malicious false rumor-mongering.

The soon-to-be-former rulers of the Holy Land of Rueda had looked rather lifeless even upon returning to their country after those events, and were in no state to make any reports for some time. Because of this, there were several days of delay before the information started to come in. Not to mention the reports were wildly inaccurate and had many omissions, exaggerations, and contradictory statements.

Among the confusion, a few of them with a keen sense for danger were able to take the opportunity to flee. However…

The remaining bishops consisted of those who weren't present when the Goddess had descended, and therefore only had skewed, inaccurate information. Not only that, but they took that flawed information and interpreted it to fit their own bias.

And so, their final conspiracy was set into motion…

"I've been looking forward to seeing you, Lady Angel!"

"Ugh!"

When we arrived at a city just before the royal capital, an unwelcome sight was awaiting us…

Yeah, *him!*

"Prince Fur Man…"

"It's Fernand!"

Well, on second thought, I guess he wasn't all that furry. Anyway…

"I'm only here to take out those who picked a fight with me. No more, no less!"

My message was loud and clear, but Fernand seemed unaffected. He was still His Royal Highness the Prince, so I had to treat him with some respect, but I didn't have to give him that courtesy in my internal monologue.

I had separated the armies of both countries; once that was done, the six of us, including Francette, myself, and the four knights Roland sent from the back moved forward, only to find Fernand waiting at the first city just before the capital. Fernand, Allan, and the man named Fa — no, Fabio — who I had met once each at the shop and Grua, the royal capital of Balmore, along with their many followers, were all there. According to them, their forces were waiting in a place some distance away from the city.

As I thought, it seemed that most of those who were cooperating with the second prince were doing so out of necessity. They couldn't publicly oppose him when the royal palace and influential aristocrats had been occupied and the first prince was missing.

I mean, if the king and first prince were out of the picture, the second prince would naturally be the official heir. Anyone who opposed this would be treated as a rebel seeking to usurp the throne and a traitor to the country. Their entire family line might end up being massacred. This was especially true when the ruler was a cruel and cowardly fool who was aware of how precarious his position was. That was why everyone just did as they were told... Until the right moment presented itself, that is.

If the first prince had died in accordance with the plan, things might have gone differently. The people could have had no choice but to give up on everything and obey the second prince, or otherwise stage a revolution, fully aware of the dishonor that would come with it...

But since Fernand was alive, they only had to wait. Justice was on their side. They could wipe out the usurper, who had committed the grave sin of murdering his own father, along with his parasitic and treacherous retainers.

And that time had finally come. A full-scale civil conflict was unlikely to break out. Everyone had only refrained from acting against the usurper out of fear for their lives, and their lack of clear justification. In a sense, he proved to be quite capable by eliminating the king and those above him in the order of succession, then effectively dividing his influential opponents before they had time to discuss how to respond, but this was likely due to input from his advisors rather than his own cunning.

At the point when he failed to kill the first prince and let him escape, his sandcastle had already begun crumbling. And so, in an attempt to take in the military, merchants, and combative aristocrats while distracting the people from their grievances, he made a reckless move to invade a friendly country. Or perhaps he was afraid the first prince would defect to the Kingdom of Balmore and try to take back the throne by force using Balmore's army.

That possibility wouldn't have been out of the question. It would have provided Balmore with a righteous cause to aid the first prince and rightful heir in his request to punish the usurper. In other words, it'd be a chance to save the people, act in the name of justice, and stand up for their ally, the Kingdom of Brancott. It was plenty of reason to invade their neighboring country, and would leave the first prince and the Kingdom of Brancott greatly in their debt.

In that scenario, which prince would the aristocrats and national army side with? It was no wonder the second prince felt threatened. And sure enough, the very thing he had feared was rapidly becoming a reality...

"Kaoru, you should rest in this city and wait for the armies of both sides to catch up. Once the forces regroup, we can attack the royal cap…"

"I'm not attacking the royal capital."

"What…?"

Why would you want to attack your own kingdom's capital? Are you stupid?!

…Yes, he was. And judging by his overly familiar attitude, Fernand seemed to think I was "that Kaoru." In other words, the Kaoru whom he had met here in Brancott.

In his mind, he had already decided that Alfa Kaoru Nagase, who he met in Balmore's royal capital, and Mifa Kaoru Nagase, who worked at the dining hall in Brancott, were one and the same, even though I kept telling him that they're two separate people…

Hmm…

"By the way, why do you keep talking to me as if we are close? I've only met you for a few minutes in Grua, correct? Do you always act so familiar with women from other countries? First you call me the Lady Angel, and the next second, I'm Kaoru? I can see why the second prince deemed you unworthy of becoming king."

"Wha! Wh-What are you…" Fernand's eyes widened in an expression of shock. Everyone around us seemed flabbergasted too.

Yeah, he deserved that. I had to keep him in check, or he would just get carried away.

"Frankly, it's quite offensive. I don't want to be near you, so please stay away. I feel like I'll become pregnant if you so much as touch me."

"Wh-Wh-Wha…"

There! I hadn't ever planned on making the armies clash or sieging the royal capital in the first place. There was no need for people to die in pointless battles, regardless of which country they were fighting for.

Military officers and aristocrats may have been happy to defeat their enemies in glorious combat, saving the capital and winning acclaim in the process, but what about those who died needlessly as a result? Maybe those who had been on the right side would be fine with it, but the soldiers on the so-called bad guy's side still had wives, children, and family members too, and they would no longer have a future.

No, I wasn't gonna have these people march into the castle as allies of justice or "the armies of the Goddess." I had already taken countermeasures to prevent this.

We had been moving forward slowly to buy more time, but we were still some distance ahead due to the support troops moving at a slower pace. Still, sending light cavalry between us and the bulk of our forces wasn't too big of an issue.

And so, we sent out Roland's four knights — also known as the Four Walls, the ones who had received the divine swords — behind the vanguard troops and Brancott's royal army to carry out my orders. The orders I gave to Brancott's armed forces were as follows:

"Choose an impressive-looking cavalry officer who's a skilled talker and send him ahead to the royal capital. Have him spread rumors among aristocrats, military personnel, civilians, everyone who'll listen; have him say that the Goddess won't forgive anyone who aids the usurper, the one who killed his own father, and that she will send forth her messenger to carry out her punishment."

The message was loud and clear: anyone who opposed me was an enemy of the Goddess and would be punished accordingly. Everyone knew about the incident that had occurred in Balmore about four years ago. How many people would try to stop me from entering the castle now? Only a heretic who didn't fear the Goddess herself would dare try. In other words, a member of the group who attacked Layette, and therefore my enemy. They would be very easy to recognize.

So, I didn't need any soldiers that wanted to achieve glory and fame through slaughter. People who were itching to kill were too dangerous to have around. My goal was to resolve this peacefully, and I didn't want that to be ruined by their ambition. No thanks!

Did I have proof that the second prince murdered the king? Well, all I said was that anyone who aided the patricidal usurper wouldn't be forgiven, and hadn't specified anyone in particular. It was more of a general statement. I mean, I think most people would agree that killing one's parents and usurping the throne were both pretty unforgivable things.

I hadn't said anything inaccurate. Nope.

"I'm afraid I might get pregnant if I stay here. We'll be moving ahead a little farther and camping out instead of staying in this city tonight."

"Yes, my lady!" "Wha...?" Francette and the Four Walls responded in unison.

And so, we moved our horses along. Fernand and the others stood there as we left them behind, the inn workers and people of the city glaring at them hatefully.

Couldn't blame them, really. They had lost the opportunity to be known as the last inn where the Angel rested before entering the royal capital, or the city that the Angel used as the headquarters for her counterattack, so of course they'd be upset.

Well, it wasn't as if this would make them think the second prince was any better than Fernand, so I didn't mind. I wanted to take a long bath before bed, but oh well. We may have been camping overnight, but I didn't mind because I still had a bed to sleep on. Tomorrow was the big day.

I would get vengeance for Layette and the orphans who had been beaten and injured, as well as the incident where they had tried to kill me. They would pay. No one will ever even think about messing with me or my friends ever again...

Chapter 44:
Final Moments

The next morning, we passed through the gates of the royal capital without issue. I mean, what gatekeeper would have even thought of stopping me? The gatekeepers of the royal capital and royal palace all knew my face, after all. Considering those rumors I'd had spread around, the second prince had to know I was coming, too.

It wasn't as if we had spread the word about the armies following behind me, but they surely would have known about them by now. They weren't stupid, and they had to be gathering their own intel. There were thousands of soldiers involved, so there had to be at least one of them leaking info for money or working in cahoots with the enemy.

But there was no sight of the enemy at the city gates. Instead…

"Hurrah! Long live the Lady Angel!!!"

"Whoa!"

They surprised me! The whole city was welcoming our arrival! That word-of-mouth had worked way too well! It would be very hard to publicly arrest me like this. In fact, that could lead to a quarrel between the soldiers and citizens…no, it could start an all-out bloodbath.

Well, it seemed most of the aristocrats and soldiers had abandoned the second prince, but those who had too much to lose or were past the point of no return…like those who were involved in the king's death…would be betting on their last chance to turn things around.

If Fernand and I were to be killed, the second prince would seize control of the situation and become ruler. The aristocrats, military, and the people had changed sides for now, but things would turn around again if the second prince was suddenly the only rightful heir.

So, their move would be…

Fwsh! Ksh!

Yup, assassination. They'd try to go for Fernand and me. Any idiot could have figured that out.

Not only did Francette have superhuman strength and vitality, but her sight, reflexes, sense of hearing, and reaction speed were off the charts. Deflecting arrows or javelins out of the sky was possible for normal soldiers, so she could practically do it with her eyes closed.

Of course, the Four Walls were capable of this as well. Not to mention, I had donned chain mail, just in case. Plate mail would have been so heavy that I would have been immobilized, but I can at least manage this much.

Besides, this was…you know. Yes, I created it as a "potion container." Thus, it was lighter, easier to move in, and more durable than normal chain mail. Stopping an arrow from a distance was no problem at all. But what if someone used a giant composite bow or ballista? Or what if I took a shot to the head? Haha… Hahaha…

I'm counting on you, Francette! I couldn't rely on the automatic defense mechanism that Celes may or may not have put on me.

I couldn't deny the possibility that the instance when the ex-bishop attacked me was just a coincidence, and I wasn't so stupid that I would just risk my life on something that wasn't even confirmed. So, I decided to consider Celes's protection unconfirmed for the moment.

Having knocked an arrow out of the air, Francette glared in the direction the projectile came from. But since it had been fired from long-range and the culprit likely hid immediately after taking the shot, there was no one to be found. Though, even if she had seen someone and chased after them, they probably would have gotten away. There would be no finding them if they'd hidden out somewhere or changed outfits and blended into the crowd. Besides, she hadn't even seen them taking the shot in the first place. It wasn't as if they had to be dressed as a soldier or anything, so they could have been in civilian clothing.

It would have been foolish to send off one of my five guards to find someone with such little hope of catching them. In fact, separating me from my guards could have been their goal in the first place. They probably assumed I had no fighting ability myself.

The events during the battle with the Aligot Empire's western invading forces were considered divine punishment for opposing the Goddess's Angel. I had deliberately set rumors in motion stating that I myself only had the ability to make healing potions.

Yeah, let's all pretend that the whole explosive potions thing didn't happen. We could all act like the Goddess made that happen directly. Though, if that had been true, no sane person would try to mess with someone so dangerous... But I mean, they were doing such stupid things *because* they weren't normal, I suppose.

Even if I wasn't here, Fernand would have eventually gathered enough forces to siege the royal capital or otherwise requested aid from other countries. That, or someone would have sacrificed their life to assassinate the second prince, or he would have been eliminated some other way rather quickly. He had already lost at the point when he failed to kill the first prince.

All I was doing was making the whole process slightly quicker, and slightly decreasing the senseless loss of life. That's all there was to it. Things might have been different if the second prince was more likeable and had enough supporters to array themselves against the first prince, but that was neither here nor there.

Anyway, we were about to arrive at the royal capital. I had been here before. It was back when that party invitation was forced upon me, so I wore a dress I had "borrowed" at the baron's house and visited this place, then switched to a maid outfit as soon as I arrived. It was quite eventful. But for some reason, there was no guard standing at the gate this time.

Maybe he had a duty to not let me pass as the gatekeeper, but he had temporarily left his post because he was afraid of being struck down by divine punishment... No, no, he was probably in the bathroom or something. Can't help it if nature calls! And so, the six of us passed through.

But man... it looked like the second prince really had been forsaken by everyone. It's pretty bad when you've even been abandoned by the gatekeeper.

But come to think of it, this should have been expected. The rightful heir to the throne, the first prince, was leading his army to the royal capital. Most of the aristocrats and military had taken his side. The merchants and commoners were all in support of the first prince. Same goes for the Temple of the Goddess.

The only ones supporting the second prince were a few aristocrats with bad reputations, some immoral merchants, and a handful of foreign bishops with dubious origins. Then there was the triple combo of rumors about "the father-killing usurper," "the wrath of the Goddess," and "the return of the Angel." I'd actually respect anyone who could still support the second prince through all that...

And so, I casually strolled farther inside. I came to realize that I was the only one who had been here before out of our party of six. Of course, I had only seen the changing room and party hall. But the others walked on as if they knew where they were going, for some reason, so I was just following them... They all knew the royal palace in their own kingdom well, so maybe they had an idea of the layouts of other palaces, too. I didn't have any choice but to shut up and follow them, anyway...

"Here."

Um, Francette? What do you mean, "here"...?

How would she have known where the king (lol) was? He could have been in his office, the bedroom, or even the dining hall. And this was...

"This is the audience chamber. This is the only place the cornered king would face his enemies."

...Did she hear that from a play or a bard's song or something? Well, I guess we were going to search every room, anyway. We may as well start with this one...

...

...

...There he is!

We opened the door, and he was actually right there.

At the far end of the room, a young man who looked like he could be the second prince sat on the throne with a crown on his head. Behind him were several bishop-looking guys. And of course, soldiers stood on guard before him. I wasn't sure if they had missed their chance to run or had some reason they couldn't leave, or maybe they were actually there out of loyalty to the king.

If they attacked, I had no choice but to beat them down. I would have to be a fool to fuss over not killing anyone at this point. The king's guards would likely be skilled fighters, but I highly doubted they would be any match for Francette wielding a divine sword, or even the Four Walls. I suppose they'd be lucky if they managed to survive with heavy injuries.

"Ah, you're finally here! I welcome you, Miss Angel!"

I questioned whether I heard the second prince Ghislain correctly.

"Huh?" I stood there, mouth agape, and he continued.

"I appreciate you bringing Balmore's army to me to acknowledge my rule. As a reward, I shall accept you as my queen once I emerge victorious over the Kingdom of Balmore!"

...So his despair had driven him right over the edge. On the other hand, it seemed his bishops and soldiers weren't as delusional as he was, since they all looked pretty anxious and pale in the face. The soldiers were gripping the hilts of their weapons tensely. I didn't care about the second prince that much, but I decided to proceed as planned for the rest of the audience...

"Your Highness, Prince Ghislain..."

"No, I am king now. Call me Your Majesty or King Ghislain."

"…"

It was hard dealing with people who weren't right in the head. But I had no choice but to continue…

"It's clear that you've murdered your own father, the king; attempted to kill your brother to usurp the throne; and betrayed your own ally, the Kingdom of Balmore, by trying to invade them to distract the world from your heinous crimes. What do you have to say for yourself?"

The second prince Ghislain was taken aback.

"What nonsense is this…? My brother Fernand disrespected and opposed you, Miss Kaoru the Angel. So he should be disinherited, and the throne should naturally belong to me."

He wasn't gonna deny he murdered his own father and tried to kill his brother, huh…? And Fernand called me Lady Angel, but this guy refers to me as Miss Angel, eh. Well, I wasn't sure if the automatic translation in my brain captured the nuances of Japanese honorifics accurately, but I could tell he saw himself as above me.

I mean, he did offer to take me as his queen as a "reward." Just how much stock did he put in his own worth…? That would be a terrible punishment for me…

"Well, the first prince did displease me, but you waged war on the Kingdom of Balmore, where I was staying, and broke a mutual agreement in the process. This is akin to declaring war on *me*, and an act of hostility against the Goddess. So much so that the first prince's actions are nothing at all in comparison."

"What…?" The second prince stared blankly… No, he wasn't a prince anymore. But I didn't want to call him king either, so I guess he was just "Ghislain."

"Miss Kaoru, I thought you'd forsaken the Kingdom of Balmore…"

Ah, so he really did believe that.

"No, I was just away for a short vacation. My home is still in the Kingdom of Balmore… Perhaps you've been tricked by someone?"

"What?!" Ghislain's eyes shot wide open, then he whirled around to face the bishops behind him. "Th-This isn't what you told me! Y-You all said…"

So, those were the survivors of Rueda who had started all of this. …Though, really, I already knew that as soon as I entered the room. This was odd, though. The bishops were looking pretty comfortable when they should have been feeling cornered.

True, there were a lot of royal guards standing between us and their side. They would obviously be skilled, considering they were tasked with protecting the royal family. We only had six people on our side, even if we counted me, and I have pretty much zero physical fighting ability.

But I couldn't imagine they didn't know about Fearsome Fran and the Four Walls, the guardsmen who had been granted divine swords. Not to mention my "non-physical" fighting ability…

Francette and the others were positioned with a space open in front of me, so I could make my denouncement, but they quickly shifted to a protective formation around me. Their first priority was to protect me from enemy attacks, so this wasn't surprising. And they just needed to stand in front of me and let our opponents come to us rather than chasing them around, so this was more efficient.

They positioned themselves to form something like a turtle's head and limbs, with Francette standing at the front as the "head" and me at the center, or the "shell." This way, she could mow down any enemy who approached us and capture Ghislain and the bishops after all of the soldiers had been taken care of. It would be an easy task with these five and their divine swords.

They needed some space to swing their weapons, so there was some distance between each of them. But they wouldn't let the enemy rush in between them, so there were no worries there.

And so, I walked behind Francette and toward Ghislain over the carpet laid out in a straight line...

Wham!

...I fell.

"Oww!" I suddenly fell through the floor into a drop of about four meters or so.

I did manage to land on my feet, but my ankles and knees couldn't absorb the shock all the way. I fell on my butt, and hit my coccyx really hard, damn it! Pretty sure I sprained my ankles and damaged my knees, too... Though, I could heal right up with a potion, anyway.

...But man, a trapdoor?! Going real old-school, aren't we? Francette didn't fall when she walked over it, so they must have tripped some sort of switch that had kept it from triggering after she passed through...

Though, really, a hole that was only this deep would only give me bruises and sprains at best. If they really wanted to kill me, they would have set some poisoned spikes or something down here. And there was some water pooled here, but there were also dried branches with leaves on them, some straw, and hay acting as a cushion. Maybe those were put here so I wouldn't get hurt? Just then...

Vwoosh!

"Gyaaaaaa! Hot, hot, hoooooot!!!"

I was engulfed in flames! This was oil, not water! The branches and hay weren't there to cushion my fall, but to make the oil burn all at once!

"E-Extinguisher..."

Just as I tried to create a fire extinguishing agent, a shadow fell around me. I instinctively looked up, and...

"Ah."

A big, round boulder just big enough to fit through the hole came falling onto me.

If only I had some time. If I had just a few seconds to think, maybe I could have come up with a plan. Maybe I could have made a potion container made of a durable superalloy that could hold up the boulder. It may have been possible for me to think of something like that to get me out of my situation.

But it took less than a second for the boulder to fall a mere four meters or so. Less than a second to react to the sudden turn of events while panicking and trying to put out the fire. It was far too little time to think and create a potion container.

And so...

"Yes! We finally defeated the blasphemer! Utterly crushed her into a pulp!"

"Hahahaha! I heard the knife failed to puncture her four and a half years ago when our comrade attacked her, but not even blade-proof clothing will save her from getting crushed by a boulder while suffocating in fire and being incinerated from the inside out! Even her bones shall burn to ashes!"

The bishops had been quiet this entire time, but they were now shouting with glee.

"We opened air holes so the flames won't even go out until the oil is done burning. Though I'm sure she died the moment the boulder fell on her. Haaahahaha!"

"What...?" Francette and the Four Walls stood there, speechless. But there was nothing they could do.

A round boulder had fallen right into the square hole in the ground. There was some space at each of the four corners, but it was too small for a person to fit through. Even if they managed to get down there, there was no way to move such a big boulder back through the hole. Especially not with the fire blazing like that...

"Hahaha, did you see the tick marks on the sides of the hole? We used those to measure and make sure there's only a few centimeters of space under the boulder, just enough room for the stacks of branches and hay.

"In other words, your precious 'Lady Angel,' — the minion of evil — was completely flattened. This is divine punishment for her foolish actions against us, the true servants of the Goddess. How unfortunate! This is what you get for dragging out the first prince and trying to seize control of this kingdom, you traitors! Haaahaha!"

"..." "..." "..."

Ggg... Gggggg... Gggrrrkkk...

Francette and the Four Walls gritted their teeth so hard that blood trickled down their mouths.

"Y-You bastards…" There wasn't a trace of sanity left in their eyes.

"Kill… I'll kill you… Diiiiiieeeeee!!!"

Clash!

The moment Francette raised her sword to rush forward, the bishops leaped into the hidden passageway behind them and activated something that brought metal bars down at the entrance of their escape route. The bars sank into the ground beneath them, and a metallic click sounded, locking them into place.

"These bars are made of steel. There's no removing them now that they're completely locked in. Securing an escape route is a basic military tactic, is it not? Though I suppose there's no sense in a holy man explaining this to a knight. Farewell now! Haaahaha, aaahahaha!!!"

No one knew where the escape route led to. The bishops had their faces obscured with hoods, and they could change into civilian clothing as they fled. They must have taken their fortunes with them already, so they could just live their lives in leisure in some other country…

That is, if these were just ordinary knights they were facing.

Shwing! Clink.

The steel bars were sliced through with ease. This was no surprise to everyone who knew about Francette's divine sword.

A divine sword… It wasn't just a made-up story to inspire people, or a rumor that had been blown out of proportion. Divine swords were real, and Francette was wielding one.

"Aaaaaaaaahhh!!!"

As the Four Walls rushed into the secret passageway and captured the bishops, Francette threw the full brunt of her unbridled rage and hatred against the enemy.

Four fighters against the bishops, and one against all of the royal guards. Perhaps their forces were distributed unevenly? No soldier in Balmore would even consider that. Not if that one warrior was Fearsome Fran.

She was a deity of the battlefield. A man-eating fiend. A demon queen. A tempest of rage that couldn't be described with mere words. Violence and death. Blood and flesh.

She easily sliced through enemy weapons, armor, marble pillars…and human bodies…like a hot knife through butter.

"Eeeeeeeeek!"

The lump of flesh atop the throne was making an unpleasant sound, but Francette would just deal with that later. It didn't seem to be going anywhere. No one, and nothing, was going to escape.

Those who had taken the Goddess from her and those who had blasphemed against her lady would pay.

Francette didn't think for a second that Kaoru had died. And why would she have? Kaoru was a Goddess.

But if Kaoru's body had perished, her little vacation here was at an end, and she had thus returned to her own world. That was why Francette had tried to protect Kaoru so desperately, but these idiots had ruined everything.

She realized she would probably never see Kaoru in this life again, all because of these idiots. These absolute fools.

The other soldiers had refused to oppose Kaoru and had made themselves scarce, but these men stayed with the second prince and had gotten in the way of Francette and her group. It was their fault that Kaoru had left this world. So, she would give them the one thing they deserved…

"…Die!"

Death. They were just following orders? They have wives and kids? She didn't give a single damn about any of that.

Die, die, die, die, die, die, die, die...

No one could stop Francette as she danced in a swirl of death and madness.

And just as it had been for Kaoru's group, no one tried to stop Prince Fernand as he made his way into the royal palace. When he arrived in the audience room, the first thing he saw was a pile of lifeless guards, the former bishops of Rueda — who had been beaten by the Four Walls within an inch of their lives — the second prince, Ghislain, curled up and crying on the throne, and Francette standing there carrying the spotless divine sword Exgram in her hand.

"Kaoru... Where is Kaoru?!"

"..."

No one replied to Fernand's question. It was clear that Kaoru's side had won convincingly. So why was Kaoru nowhere to be seen? And why was no one answering Fernand's question...?

An ominous, sinking feeling grew in his chest. Fernand had opted to deliberately avoid mentioning the obviously out-of-place sight in his view. He felt as if there was no turning back once he asked about it.

Indeed, in the center of the floor leading from the entrance of the audience room to the throne, there was a hole with smoke and heat coming out of it...

Just then, a ball of light appeared in the space right between Fernand and Francette, then rapidly expanded and took on a humanoid shape. It was the being that Francette had met twice already, and the Four Walls had met once before.

The Goddess Celestine had descended.

"I can't detect Kaoru's soul anymore! Where... Where is Kaoru?!"

61

Celestine had set up Kaoru with an automatically-activated barrier and a system that would automatically strike back at her assailants. However, those were specifically designed to deal with surprise attacks and long-range shots. They were meant to protect Kaoru from swords, spears, arrows, and other weapons that could suddenly take her out.

If this had been Earth, Celestine may have granted Kaoru protections against guns, grenades, rocket launchers, and maybe even things like cannons, fuel-air explosives, bunker busters, or even a nuke. But such things didn't exist in this world. That was why Celestine had set countermeasures in place to protect Kaoru from realistic surprise attacks. There was no point in granting her protection from nuclear weapons that didn't exist.

As long as she wasn't killed instantly, she could create a potion (along with its container) within seconds to deal with the threat and heal herself. And since she was more useful alive than dead, there was no reason for anyone to kill her outright. This was Celestine's line of thinking, and thus she underestimated the potential danger Kaoru could find herself in.

The bishops who had survived the fall of Rueda must have done research on the incident when one of the other former bishops had attacked Kaoru with a dagger, and thus learned that she had somehow protected herself from the weapon. And so, they had devised a second and third layer of attacks in order to kill her, even if she was able to protect herself from a dagger or some arrows.

External burns, lung damage through breathing in the heat, suffocation from the lack of oxygen, and even being crushed by a giant boulder. Since the bishops assumed Kaoru was a normal human who had been bestowed with a small blessing from the Goddess

Celestine, and not a goddess herself, they had been confident in their ability to kill her, and they had been right about that.

One of the Four Walls pointed wordlessly in response to Celestine's words of panic. His finger indicated the hole in the ground.

"What...?"

A hole that shouldn't have been there... Celestine didn't think it was anything worth noticing and had ignored it completely, but stared at it now in a fluster...

"Nothing... I don't sense Kaoru's soul or consciousness... Nothing at all... Not even when I expand my range of detection... Ahhh, I wanted to drag it out for at least 400 to 500...hopefully 4,000 to 5,000 years! But five?! She's gone after less than five measly years?!"

Once a human's body perished, their immaterial presence dispersed and vanished. That is, unless a being like Celestine or the other deities happened to be around to protect them or made preparations to protect them in anticipation of their death. Celestine hadn't expected Kaoru's body to be destroyed so abruptly, so it took her some time to realize what had happened. By the time she noticed Kaoru's soul and consciousness had disappeared, it was already too late.

"My precious Kaoru... He entrusted me with her care... I owed her so much... And she was my first friend... Unforgivable! This is unforgivable!!! I'll destroy this entire kingdom...no, this entire continent! I'll burn it to ashes and banish it to the depths of the sea for all eternity! I'll make sure I never catch sight of it again, so I can forget all about this unpleasant emotion welling up inside me..."

Everyone froze, then the despair set in. Not only was the Kingdom of Brancott in peril, but so was every other country on the continent. Every human and every life form on this vast landmass would meet their doom. The Goddess herself had announced the execution, a death sentence that couldn't be overruled.

"Despair" was the only word that could adequately describe the emotion within everyone in the room.

If it had been Celestine's main body, or even an offspring that had been set to a slightly higher level, she may not have been quite so enraged. But unfortunately, this Celestine had her ability to think adjusted to a lower limit to make it possible to communicate with humans, which also gave her emotions particular to lower life forms, such as anger and hatred. It was only a little bit...

But that little bit of dark emotion inside her was now going berserk. There was nothing that could be done...

"Please wait!"

As everyone stood immobilized by the intense pressure emanating from Celestine's body, one person recklessly attempted to stop the Goddess.

"You're..."

"Yes, I am Lady Kaoru's guardian knight, Francette!"

Celestine glared at Francette.

"You're the one who was acting all high and mighty during that one distortion incident..."

"Urgh!"

She had been listening quietly with Kaoru there, but she must have been quite annoyed, considering she still held a grudge over it.

"So, what sort of entertaining lecture does this lowlife who unashamedly calls herself a 'guardian knight,' despite failing to protect Kaoru, have in store for me?"

She's really maaad!

Fernand and the Four Walls trembled in fear at her response, but the continent was already doomed. It wasn't as if things could get any worse. Unless Celestine decided to destroy not just this continent, but the entire world, that is…

But it was hard to believe the Goddess would go *that* far, no matter how enraged she was…

As such, no one attempted to stop Francette. After all, they were both devotees of Kaoru, each lost in their anger. Maybe they could reach an understanding. It wasn't completely out of the question. They all watched with the faintest of hopes in their hearts…

"Lady Kaoru wouldn't want this! Lady Kaoru may be unforgiving to those who mean to do her harm, but she has always shown mercy to the innocent, even if they were from an enemy country. She would never wish for the deaths of so many innocent people and those who were close to her! I'm certain she would be very sad if she heard of this… The entire reason Lady Kaoru came here in the first place was to try and reduce the number of senseless deaths to a minimum. If her efforts are not only nullified, but if even more people were to die…"

"Urgh…" Celestine recoiled at Francette's words. She didn't care at all for lower life forms, but she knew that Kaoru had a special place in her heart for them. Even now that she was dead, she still wanted to honor Kaoru's will for being her friend and helping with "that person" in so many ways.

Celestine knew Kaoru had died — perished completely, in other words — but Francette thought Kaoru had just lost her temporary, mortal form in this world and had returned to her own. Due to that belief, she was able to calm herself from her temporary burst of anger. Since she was the only one with somewhat of a tolerance built up against Celestine, she felt a duty and desperate need to calm the Goddess herself.

After all, the fate of all living creatures in the entire continent rested on her shoulders...

"Please consider Lady Kaoru's kindness and have mercy..." Francette knelt as she made her request, and the others followed in a fluster.

"...Very well. I will be considerate of Kaoru's will. I won't hurt anyone."

Fernand, the Four Walls, and Francette were filled with absolute joy at Celestine's words. Though, rather than let it show outwardly, they kept their emotions in check...

They had all been prepared to die here today, but now they only wished for no harm to come to the people of their kingdom and the other countries. If someone had to die as punishment for what had taken place, they wanted to be the only ones to pay the price.

"Thank you, O great Goddess! Now, we offer you our lives in hopes of soothing your anger..." Francette said and switched from a kneeling to a sitting position, and the others followed suit. It seemed they did so to avoid falling into an awkward position after the Goddess took their lives.

But in response...

"You fool! After all that talk of going against Kaoru's will and how sad she would be, you suggest I kill her most trusted allies? ... Are you an idiot?"

Celestine was right. Francette slumped her shoulders, disappointed at her own stupidity.

"Enough! I will leave it up to you all to dispose of the cause of all this. Don't you dare let a single one of them escape!"

With that, Celestine disappeared. Now that Kaoru was gone, most of Celestine's interest in the individuals of this world had vanished with her. And just as before, she would likely go back to quietly working on dealing with distortions without getting involved with humans in general. Just as she had before Kaoru had arrived in this world…

"…"

Francette, the Four Walls, and Fernand all looked rather dreadful. The ex-bishops of Rueda had been left groaning on the ground, and Ghislain still sat on the throne, muttering to himself that he had been saved, despite the fact that he hadn't been saved at all…

"…Am I to report what happened here to Sir Roland, His Majesty, and the people of the kingdom? And to Emile, Belle, Layette, and the others… Although the loss of many lives is unavoidable in war, the price we paid was far too high…"

The Four Walls, Fernand, and his companions just hung their heads, at a loss for words.

"So I died, huh…"

A place of nothing but whiteness. I had been here once before.

"It's been quite a while."

The young man in white clothing appeared before me. The self-proclaimed God-like being, who was actually a highly advanced life form that made humans look like water fleas in comparison… supposedly.

"How is Kyoko doing?"

"She's well, though she's getting older and has been spending most of her time in bed as of late…"

She was my classmate, so I knew her age, even if we hadn't contacted each other lately. That was mostly because neither of us could move from our beds. That was especially true in my case, what with all the IVs and the oxygen tanks and everything…

So, I would be leaving first…

"How is Kaoru doing?"

The God-like being suddenly lowered his head in response to my question.

"I'm terribly sorry! Miss Kaoru Nagase has passed away..."

"What...?"

Impossible!

"How?! I thought she had the blessing of the Goddess of that world! She was supposed to be immune to illnesses, injury, and old age! What happened?!" I asked for an explanation, and he filled me in on what had happened.

"So, Kaoru wasn't able to reincarnate again and vanished completely... In other words, she's dead?"

"...Yes. I'm so sorry... I regret to tell you that your reason for reincarnating in that world is now gone. If you'd like, as a token of apology, I could have you choose from any of the other worlds and reincarnate there..."

"No, I'd like to go to Kaoru's world as planned. I'm not interested in any other option."

"B-But Miss Kaoru is already..."

"Even still!"

I didn't back down.

"Because I'm Reiko Kuon. I'm Kaoru Nagase's friend! No matter how far apart we may be, no matter how many decades have passed... And even if Kaoru has passed away... There's only one place for me to go. To Verny, the world where Kaoru went!"

With that, I mustered a fierce smile. I didn't believe it for one second. Kaoru Nagase couldn't have died twice so easily. Even if I had heard it directly from God himself.

"Please forgive meeeeee!!!"

I didn't know where she'd learned it from, but the Goddess prostrated herself before me in a classic Japanese gesture of apology.

Well, I already knew why. That godlike being managing Earth had already told me everything.

"For starters, I'd like my body to be reincarnated with the same conditions as Kaoru, along with an Item Box and the ability to understand every language. That is the basic loadout, right? And for my bonus cheat power, I'd like to have unlimited magical powers!"

"Gyaaaaaa! She's completely shameless!!!"

Chapter 45:
Return

"Shameless? You're calling *me* shameless when I'm asking for the minimum required powers to find Kaoru, in *your* stead, after *you* lost sight of her and didn't even bother to search?"

"Uhh… Wait, what? Find Kaoru? But her soul and presence are completely gone now…"

"You're not the one who gets to decide that. It isn't as if you confirmed that in the Akashic Records, right?"

"Oh, well, no. A lesser being of my level doesn't have access to the Akashic Records… Though, my main body could check them if absolutely necessary… I can only look up very limited and simple records pertaining to this specific planet."

It was just as the Earth God had said.

"Then there's a chance. The possibility isn't zero."

"…"

The Goddess grew silent.

"Can you please tell me what you know and explain how it happened?"

"…V-Very well…"

Regarding the bonus perks, it seemed like she had vaguely agreed with my terms…right? Okay, then. I'll show everyone that the Kuon family doesn't know what it means to give up!

"So, this is the alternate world of Verny. The world where Kaoru is…"

Yes, it's the world where she *is*, not where she *was*. We won't ever give up, no matter what happens…

And off in the distance, I could see the capital of the Kingdom of Brancott, Aras. The place where Kaoru disappeared…

All right, time to test out my powers!

If I tried using magic without practicing first, it could end pretty badly. Really, though, this so-called "magic" was supposedly just an explicable phenomenon backed by science. It wasn't as if magical fairies were going to appear or anything. I didn't know how exactly it was scientific, but you know what they say… "Any sufficiently advanced technology is indistinguishable from magic."

I decided not to think too deeply about it.

"Water Ball…"

Whoa, a blob of water appeared! This means I don't need to carry a canteen around or worry about dying of thirst!

"Fire Ball…"

Good, I could use this for cooking and prevent myself from freezing to death! And now…

"Darkness beyond twilight, crimson beyond blood that flows…"

…Nope, nothing happened!

Those mountains in the distance had a huge hole gouged out of them before I got here! Yes, I'm sure that's it.

Now, off to the royal capital I go!

I paid the gate guard three silver coins and made it into the royal capital of Aras safely. This value of three silver coins supposedly hadn't changed for a long time, and neither had the price of admission. And so, I continued straight ahead toward the royal palace.

Of course, a commoner couldn't just waltz into the royal palace... Unless you went through a specific section, that is. Indeed, it was the area known as the Sacred Ground.

Lady Kaoru the Angel... Also known as the Goddess of another world by a select few... Sheesh, just what was that girl doing...?

Anyway, the Sacred Ground was the place where Kaoru had sacrificed herself and ascended to the heavens to prevent a war between the Kingdoms of Balmore and Brancott. The boulder that was said to have crushed Kaoru had fit perfectly into the hole in the ground, making it impossible to remove by lifting it out. They did manage to open a hole that was about the same size next to it and roll the boulder aside, but they only found her unrecognizable, carbonized remains...

Those ashes were still carefully preserved as holy relics.

Only the route leading to the Sacred Ground was open for visitors to enter freely, though it was surrounded by strong walls.

The building that included the former audience room was now treated like a temple, and a new building had been constructed next to it to be used as a new palace, with a replacement audience room.

I slipped in with the general visitors and observed the Sacred Ground for some time, then left the royal palace. I had to secure an inn and get some food, of course. My work would come after everyone went to bed.

Late into the night...

I quietly left the inn and went into the royal palace. The Sacred Ground was open during the day, but it was understandably closed off after dark. Fortunately, such security measures were completely pointless in the face of magic.

"Invisibility Field!"

A spell that made me vanish...though, there was probably a scientific explanation for how it worked, like enabling visible light to pass through my body or bending space somehow. Whatever it did, it allowed me to be completely undetectable to the naked eye, and I walked right past the soldiers and into the building.

I used magic to open the locked door, then pushed it open just enough to slip inside. Once I was inside the empty building, I used magic to allow myself to see in the dark. Then I continued toward the "Sacred Room"...

"Let's see..."

There were no soldiers standing guard inside the building, so I could get away with making some comments to myself.

The exterior was well-guarded enough, and no one would try to sneak into the Sacred Ground to steal anything, anyway. This was a world where the Goddess existed, after all. And a goddess that could be somewhat harsh against people who annoyed her, at that.

The god of Earth had only heard a secondhand report from the goddess of this world, Lady Celestine, and she was in such a depressed and fretful state that she could hardly explain what had happened. As such, he'd had to piece together bits and pieces of information that she managed to get out. It seemed the Goddess Celestine wasn't the most articulate.

According to her, Kaoru's soul and presence had completely vanished, and couldn't be detected even after widening her search range. She had thus concluded that Kaoru was gone for good, but…

This was coming from someone who had only known Kaoru for less than five years or so. In other words, it was too hasty a decision, given that it involved Kaoru. She would never die and leave us behind like that. Just like she had last time…

Kaoru will surely be waiting for us…

I had heard everything. I asked questions over and over, right down to the finest of details. About the body and powers that Kaoru had acquired… And the specifics of the situation when the incident had occurred.

At that moment, what would Kaoru have done? After thinking through it for so long, I had reached a conclusion.

Where was the spot where it was last opened? It was only natural to assume that whatever was closest to the spot where it was opened would be the last thing that was put in there.

So…

"Time-space oscillation magic! Create a tremor through dimensions to force open dimensional storage (Item Box) synced to someone else's psychic waves! Open, dimensional door!"

Vwoom…

A tremble ran through space, causing the world to distort. Then, a giant dimensional tremor shook reality itself…

"Is this the source of the distortion?!"

A goddess suddenly appeared with an intense look on her face, and…

Poof! A girl appeared.

She looked to be about twelve years old. (By this world's standards.) The girl had remarkably scary-looking eyes. Not to mention…

"Gyaaaaaa! It…it buuuuuurns!!!"

The girl was on fire, her entire body engulfed in the flames.

"Fire extinguishing potion, come ouuut!"

"Supersized Water Baaaaaall!"

"Kyaaaaaa! W-W-Waaateeer!!!"

Splaaaaaaash!

The girl with the scary eyes was washed away in a massive flood of water and disappeared somewhere…

"K-K-Kaoruuuuuu!"

"I knew you'd come for me, Celes! I had no time to think of a way out, but I was able to escape into the Item Box without hesitation because I trusted you. Time is frozen in the Item Box, so there was no way for me to get out on my own..."

It had already been proven that Kaoru's Item Box could store living creatures during the Aligot Empire's invasion, when it stored Belle as she dove into the well. A bead of sweat rolled down Celestine's forehead as she embraced Kaoru and let out a cry of joy. It was likely that her body didn't actually produce sweat, but it had such functions as a medium of expression...

"O-O-Of course! I-I-I would never give up on you so easily and l-leave you alone..." Celestine said with a tight smile, but she could clearly see the lip movements of the girl standing behind Kaoru...

"You. Owe. Me. Big. For. This..."

Gyaaaaaa!!!

Celestine was thus deeply indebted to a girl who had demanded so many unreasonable perks, and so shamelessly, at that...

But she couldn't let Kaoru learn that she had actually given up on finding her, and that she would have been stuck in the Item Box for all eternity without Reiko's help. She absolutely couldn't find out about this! And so, although it was likely that she would pay greatly for this debt, Celestine had no choice but to be at the mercy of the other girl, who was playing along for now.

"I'll have to do something about these burnt-up, soaking clothes…"

The injuries from when Kaoru had fallen through the hole and gotten torched had already been healed using potions. Her hair, which had been singed pretty badly, was already fixed, as well. Normally, her burns should have been of such severity that she would have been in critical condition, but the shield that Celestine had bestowed on her had contained the damage.

Then, Kaoru finally noticed the other person standing there.

"Wait…"

She recognized this girl. It had been a little under a year for her, but it felt as if it had been over a decade since they last met. But no matter how many years went by, there was no way she could forget. She was one of the only two close friends she had. There was no mistaking her.

"…Reiko…as a high schooler…"

It was Reiko Kuon in her fifteen-year-old body, just like Kaoru. One of her two best friends. Compared to Kaoru, Reiko's body was rather well developed… Particularly certain parts of her body. So, Kaoru thought Reiko was currently the high school version of herself, but since her body was that of a fifteen-year-old, it was technically her middle school version.

"Hehe… I'm here…"

"Reikoooooo!!!"

Reiko believed she would see Kaoru again, but this was completely out of the blue for Kaoru. She couldn't help but scream and embrace her old friend. And having been hugged by Kaoru in her soaking wet clothes, Reiko also ended up being drenched.

"I'm sure you two have a lot to talk about, but we should leave this place. There are many humans on the way."

"Oh…"

The guards would be rushing over to see what the commotion was about. Water did just flood out of the building, after all.

"Repair, clean, and dry!"

Celestine repaired the damage caused by the flood, cleaned up all the dirt, and dried everything off, erasing all traces of what had just happened here. Kaoru's clothes were blessed with the same effect, leaving them looking good as new. Reiko's clothes, which had gotten wet from Kaoru, were dried as well.

But there wasn't enough time to deal with the water that had flooded out of the building, so that was left as it was.

"Transporting!"

Then they were gone.

When the guards arrived on the scene, they were puzzled to find the Sacred Ground unchanged despite having so much water around the building. Afterward, the priests surmised that Lady Celestine, who hadn't made an appearance since the incident, had cried tears of anguish for her late friend, and everyone agreed with that theory.

"Well, I'm off to give him the good news!" Celestine vanished, having transported Kaoru and Reiko outside of the city, then to an inn as per Reiko's request.

No time had passed at all since the incident from Kaoru's point of view, and Celestine had no intention of talking about what had happened during her absence. And so, the most important thing for Celestine now was to see "him" again and fill him in on the events.

Kaoru and Reiko were left alone together. They also had a room for two, so they could talk until morning without interruption.

"R-Reiko, why are you here...? And you look..." Kaoru asked, and Reiko responded rather casually.

"I'm in the same boat as you. I died, then that godlike manager of Earth reincarnated me."

"What...?"

Kaoru had suspected that this was the case ever since she saw Reiko in her younger form. There was simply no other explanation. But...

"That guy said he only makes mistakes once every several thousand years, and he made another one already?! And with my friend, of all people..." Kaoru said through gritted teeth.

"Oh, no, no! He didn't make a mistake or anything. I got to live a full life!"

"Huh? But how'd you die so quickly...? Did you get in an accident or something? Or was it fate?"

"No, I died of old age."

"...Huh? What? Whaaaaaaaaat?!"

"...So that much time has already passed on Earth... Maybe time flows differently there compared to this world..."

"Huh? No, the god of Earth said time passes at the same rate."

"Huh?"

"I'm saying the same amount of time should have passed since you reincarnated here, Kaoru..."

"Whaaat?"

"Lady Celestine said herself that it's been over seventy years since you disappeared…"

"Whaaaaaaaaat?!" Kaoru was dumbfounded. "H-H-How did this happen… That Celes… I thought she rescued me from the Item Box right away… Wait. When I was freed, you were there. And decades had already passed. That means… Celes. Celeeeeees!!!"

The cat was out of the bag. She knew everything. But it couldn't be helped. It would have been impossible to keep it a secret forever…

The next day, the two girls left the royal capital. Their destination was Grua, the royal capital of Balmore. There were many things Kaoru had to confirm there…

All the people she wanted to protect and take care of… What could have happened to them in her absence? She had to see the truth with her own eyes. She also wanted to know what had happened after the incident.

But all of that had happened in the distant past, over seventy years ago. Most of those involved were likely dead already. Through being executed, or perhaps due to old age…

So, those things could wait. The average human lifespan was very short in this world. It wasn't just infants and mothers giving birth who had high death rates, but adult males died pretty often, too. And that was without counting the massive deaths caused during war.

Therefore, the chances of Kaoru's acquaintances being alive were rather slim. If even a tenth of them were still alive, that would have been quite impressive.

But she had to know. What sort of life had they led since her disappearance? So many children she wanted to protect but couldn't... So many people she had helped who never got the chance to repay her... She had to know what had happened to them...

"Let's set up camp," Kaoru said to Reiko.

"Right. We should go somewhere that can't be seen from the road, then."

And so, the two moved away from the road, toward a spot where they wouldn't be targeted by any dubious strangers, and...

Poof! Kaoru popped a tent out from the Item Box.

"Oh, I haven't put anything in mine yet. I should stock up on water, food, and other essentials while I can..."

"Huh?" Kaoru looked surprised by Reiko's comment. "...You have an Item Box, too?"

"Yeah. Oh, I can make water, but it's kind of a pain to use magic each time. It'd be more convenient if I could pop it out of my Item Box in a container already..."

"Yeah, I know what you...wait, you can make potions too?! You totally copied me!"

Kaoru looked rather sullen, considering she had put a lot of thought into her ability. Besides, that would mean they had the same exact schtick. It wasn't as if it would cause her any inconvenience, but...

"Oh, no, I got a different ability. I can use magic, without any limits…"

"That's cheating!"

"Look who's talking, Kaoru!"

And so, Kaoru learned through Reiko about what had happened on Earth since she had departed…

However, Kaoru had made sure first to tell her friend not to mention anything about the Nagase family. She would never get to see them again. If they were in distress, there was nothing she could do. It was too late to help, no matter what misfortune awaited them. She could have healed any of their injuries or illnesses if she was able to see them now, but they were all so far away…

And so, it was much better to remain ignorant and assume that they had lived happy lives. Besides, if they were ever in real danger, there was a chance that the Earth God had given them a bit of a helping hand to atone for his mistake. It was best to believe that was true.

To those who lived in that world, Kaoru was someone who was long deceased. She had already said her goodbyes. The image of her family in her mind was better left untouched. It was completely normal for Kaoru to think this way.

"…So why did you come chasing after me…?"

"What's that supposed to mean?!" Reiko objected to Kaoru's comment. "Isn't it obvious? Because…"

"Because what?"

"Because I, Reiko Kuon, am Kaoru Nagase's best friend!"

"…Dummy."

And so, they went on to exchange more information.

"Whaaaaaat?! Kyo is coming too?!"

"Yeah. You can't keep the trio separated, ya know?"

Kyoko was your average modern girl. Kaoru was a considerate quick thinker, but was often thought to be scary looking because of her eyes. And then there was Reiko, who could be quite cutting and sharp tongued, despite her seemingly gentle and nerdy appearance.

No obnoxious boys, con artists, perverted teachers, or bullying upperclassmen stood a chance when the three of them were together. Their classmates and younger female students relied on them, and they crushed all evil in their path!

"We are KKR, the guardians of our academy!"

As an aside, the name "KKR" came from combining the first letters from Kaoru, Kyoko, and Reiko's names.

"Gyaaaaaa!!!"

The catchphrase was from a few years ago for Kaoru, and a few decades ago for Reiko, and they rolled around with their heads in their hands as they remembered it with embarrassment.

"*...Haah...haah...* That was pretty brutal..."

"I thought I was gonna die..."

Kaoru and Reiko finally managed to compose themselves after taking massive psychic damage.

"...But Reiko, you're an old lady, aren't you? I can see why your appearance changed, but why do you still act and sound like your younger self?" Kaoru asked.

Reiko responded in a casual tone, "Oh, that? I was wondering the same thing, so I asked the Earth God. According to him, a presence can become exhausted from deterioration due to wear and tear on the body and mind. In other words, it gets weaker when your heart gets worn down, or as your body and brain degrade over time."

"And when you die, you're removed from your physical body. Normally, your soul and presence disperse right away, but..."

"We were salvaged before that happened?"

"Yup. And they refueled our discarnate entity with some sort of energy, which is why we're so lively! It's kind of like when you take the CPU out of an older PC, clean it up, then move it into a new build... Though, Kaoru, I guess in your case, that wasn't really necessary, so you got reincarnated directly.

"Anyway, I guess I have the same energy as I did when I was young, but with several decades worth of knowledge. I knew I'd be coming to this world, so I did a lot of studying to prepare, too. Chemistry, physics, mechanical engineering, political economy, agriculture, and more... So...now, I guess I'm..."

"...A loli hag?" Kaoru asked.

"Look who's talking..." Reiko shot back.

"Urrrgh..."

"...Aha."

"Haha."

"Ahahahahaha!!!"

No matter how many years went by, Reiko was still Reiko. One of Kaoru's only two best friends…

"Oh, you still have your glasses?"

"Yeah. But I had my vision fixed, of course, so these don't have any prescription in them."

"Huh? Then why are you wearing them?"

"Because…"

"Because?"

"Because I look cooler with them on!" Reiko exclaimed.

"…"

But Kaoru had a feeling this was for her sake. Things had been like this for over ten years, ever since middle school. Reiko wore her glasses, and Kaoru had her scary eyes. That was probably why she was still wearing them for their reunion…

Kaoru's eyes were probably as scary looking as ever, too.

"Shaddap!!!" Kaoru suddenly burst out, and Reiko smiled warmly.

She could tell what her old friend was thinking. They had been so close for so long, after all.

And so, their conversation went on.

"About what we talked about earlier…" Reiko began.

"Huh? Which part?"

"The incident about the Goddess leaving you alone."

"Ah…"

"Think you could not bring that up with her?"

"What? Why? I was gonna give her an earful when I see her next…" Kaoru asked in confusion.

"Well, I could use it as leverage for future negotiations…"

"I see… Oh, you're bad."

"Heheheh…"

These two were dangerous together. They were relatively harmless individually, but they were a recipe for disaster when combined. Such was the nature of KKR, the guardians of the academy...

"First, I wanna go back to Grua and check if everyone is...no, that might be a bit difficult. I just want to check if the people I know that are still alive aren't in some horrible situation, then go to the library and look up what happened in my absence. Then..."

"Then?" Reiko asked.

Kaoru grinned.

"If anyone used the chaos of the situation to try anything funny... Well, most of them are probably dead or have pretty much lived a full life by now... Damn, they would've gotten away with it by now... I guess the best I could do is demolish their houses, denounce their family names, and turn their descendants into penniless commoners...

"Aristocrats and royalty really seem to care about the reputation and continuation of their family names, and bloodlines and all that jazz, so I'll just drag them through the mud — no, through the manure — for what they've done..."

"Agreed... Some might argue that their children and grandchildren had nothing to do with it, but it's not like they're being punished that much. We'd just be taking back what their ancestors took through unjust means. They never deserved their fortune and reputation in the first place..."

Kaoru had always hated those who trampled upon the weak or lied and stole from others. She didn't mind lying to protect others or to make them happy, but malicious and hurtful lies and lies told to profit oneself were out of the question.

Though, she didn't often directly reproach those who did tell such lies. Instead, she classified them as enemies in her mind, and when it came to dealing with enemies, anything was fair game. Of course, that included lying to them without mercy, just as they had done.

Kaoru had learned to hold back somewhat by the time she became a working adult. She hadn't been a child anymore, after all. But when she was a student, a child who could still get away with things due to her youth, she went all out along with Reiko and Kyoko...

And from Reiko's point of view, the Kaoru she knew was 99% composed of Kaoru as a student.

"If your friends are still alive, are you going to reveal yourself?"

"No..." Kaoru shook her head. "In the end, I failed to protect them... And now that they're finally free from being bound by their Goddess and are off living their own lives, I don't think showing myself will do them any good..."

In this world, the average lifespan was quite short. Kaoru figured that if any of them were still alive, it would likely just be the members of the Eyes of the Goddess, who were younger than her. Besides, the others were adults, all of them older than Kaoru, so it wasn't as if they needed her to take care of them. Those children were the only people Kaoru felt responsible for. She had given Francette more than enough in the way of blessings, so if she had lived an unfortunate life, it was her own fault. Kaoru couldn't do everything for her.

Though, it could also be said that most of the orphans would have died within a few years if they hadn't met Kaoru, considering their health and general circumstances at the time. One could say that they should have been grateful for being able to live happily for the few years they had before Kaoru's disappearance, but she couldn't see it that way. Since she had gotten involved with them and decided to protect them, she intended to watch over them until the end.

But if she was to watch over them until "the end," it could be said that she had fulfilled her duty already...

"I'll sneak a peek at them from hiding and leave if they look happy," Kaoru decided.

Reiko didn't ask what Kaoru was going to do if they didn't look happy. She already knew the answer.

"Come to think of it, there is one unanswered question..."

"Huh? What is it?" Reiko asked, but most of what she had asked Celestine involved Kaoru's disappearance, so she didn't know much relating to the kingdom of Kaoru's acquaintances.

"About the hole I fell through and the boulder that was dropped on top of me... I guess you could have dug four meters or so if you got a bunch of people to dig all day and night, then switch out people as they got exhausted... But that boulder! That thing was almost perfectly round! It must've been pretty hard to shave down such a big boulder so it fitted that hole perfectly in such a short time. I wonder how they did it..."

"Oh, I know how."

"What?!"

Kaoru had voiced her question out loud, but didn't actually expect Reiko to know the answer.

"Around noon yesterday, I went on the Sacred Ground tour as a tourist and the tour guide answered that very question. Supposedly, that boulder was already at the Temple of the Goddess, next to the Goddess statue. Someone who understood that this world is round put it there to represent the world being watched over by the Goddess. Either the culprits decided to use it by sheer chance, or maybe they wanted to kill the Angel with something from the Temple of the Goddess out of a twisted sense of irony."

"What? But how could it fit the hole so perfectly by coincidence…?"

"It's the other way around. They dug the hole to fit the size of the boulder. Duh!"

"Ah…" Kaoru had judged it completely wrong. "But that huge boulder was so smooth, like a perfect sphere… It must have taken a bunch of stonemasons or those bishops themselves a lot of manual labor. Can't you just picture them…?"

"Scrubbing it?"

Gyahahaha!!!

In the darkness, two young girls (by appearance, at least) could be heard laughing. How wonderful it was to have someone who shared the same sense of humor…

It warmed Kaoru's heart to be able to joke around in Japanese for the first time in many years. Of course, since she had mastery over the language of this world, she could crack jokes in the native tongue here, too…

But no one found those jokes amusing. At all. Even the orphans just looked at her as if they were troubled. As if they were asking themselves, "Do I really have to laugh…?" As if to say, "A Goddess shouldn't say such senseless things." Their tight expressions made it clear they were forcing themselves to try to laugh.

And so, Kaoru had shouted, "…Urgh, just kill me!!!"

Differences in culture were quite difficult to overcome…

The two headed for Grua, the capital of Balmore, on foot. There were quite a lot of stagecoaches going around, but they wouldn't be able to speak freely while riding one.

Their topics of conversation involved events in Japan, things that happened before Kaoru entered the Item Box, Celestine, and the direction they would be taking from here on… None of which could be discussed in front of others.

Having just recently reunited in this world, it was impossible for them to fill several days' worth of entertaining conversation with topics that would be fine for others to hear.

Kaoru still had her chariot in her Item Box, but she didn't feel like buying a horse, nor did she want to ride through the city streets in that distinctive carriage. It stood out like nothing else, and there was a chance that someone was still alive to recognize it. But, really, the main reason she didn't want to use it was sentimental in nature.

Ed isn't around anymore…

Indeed, horses lived rather short lives. Kaoru's beloved horse, Ed, must have passed away, still waiting for Kaoru without ever knowing why she had left.

Ed, her old partner and brother-in-arms. He was gone forever…

"So, we made it to the royal capital…"

The two had arrived at the royal capital, Grua. Of course, Kaoru had changed her hair and eye color with potions and switched over to a less conspicuous outfit. It wasn't as if she only had her favorite outfit, which had become a trademark of sorts. Her more normal clothes were stored in the Item Box, so they hadn't degraded a bit.

…The style was a bit dated, by seventy years or so, but that wasn't a big issue. Probably.

Most of the people who had met Kaoru were gone by now. She just needed to look out for particularly old people, and if they had only seen her a couple times, over seventy years ago, it was unlikely that anyone would recognize her face.

Plus, Kaoru was generally understood to not be a goddess, but rather a human who had received the blessing of the Goddess, also known as the Angel. Despite her nickname, she wasn't thought of as a literal angel or spirit, something in the same realm as the Goddess.

Therefore, the only people who might have thought that Kaoru's appearance would remain the same throughout all these years were the ones who thought she was a goddess, like Francette or the Eyes of the Goddess. The likelihood of being recognized was slim to none.

"Call me Kaoru from now on, okay? I'm not Nagase Kaoru or Kaoru from Japan, but Kaoru, a resident of this world. The girl you knew named Kaoru doesn't exist anymore… Besides, people will think I'm an aristocrat if you refer to me by my family name."

"…Got it. Then I'll be just Reiko, too. I'll live in this new world with my new name and life!"

That was the Reiko she'd always known. She was quick to catch on.

The name Kaoru had spread far and wide by the time she had put herself in the Item Box. It had become quite common for people to name their daughters Kaoru, after the girl who was loved by the Goddess. As such, that name was already popular, having been bestowed upon girls ranging from newborn children to ladies in their mid-seventies, so it wouldn't have at all been suspicious for her to call herself Kaoru. In other words, there was no need to go by an alias.

"First, let's find ourselves an inn. Camping out in a tent while traveling is one thing, but it's not like we can do that in the middle of the royal capital. We'll be in trouble if we end up with no good place to stay."

Reiko agreed, and the two set out to find an inn.

Reiko had already procured funds from Celestine. It was completely legitimate currency, rather than some fake money that Celestine had created. According to Celestine, it had been "completely removed from human ownership."

...Probably taken from a chest in a sunken ship, or something like that.

It was likely that she could have created money out of thin air, but that probably went against her own personal policy. Of course, Kaoru's Item Box was still full of money that she had earned a long time ago, but to her surprise, the currency had changed during the past seventy years. Plus, several neighboring countries were now using the same unified coinage...

It couldn't be used throughout the entire continent, but it was accepted in the Kingdoms of Balmore, Brancott, Aseed, and the Aligot Empire. Someone could even use it for pretty much the same value in Drisard and the Kingdom of Jusral, which bordered the Kingdom of Brancott.

Coins were minted in their own respective countries, of course, but the composition of gold or silver, along with their weight, were strictly regulated and standardized, so they could be used across regions with the same value.

Normally, in Kaoru's world, currency fluctuated in value based on the credit of the country where it was minted, rather than by the gold and silver content. This world hadn't reached that point yet in most places, but these four countries had established a stable commercial sphere, which was quite a feat.

"...So, this is the currency they use now..." Reiko said after they secured their inn and produced a drawstring pouch.

She pulled out a bronze coin, a small silver coin, a silver coin, a small gold coin, and a gold coin, the five types that were commonly used. Other coins did exist, but they were used in large transactions between merchants or in international trade, and most commoners never saw them in person.

Kaoru stared at the coins Reiko laid out in front of her. It seemed all of them had the same design, with someone's face on the front. But the angle and expression were different on each coin, and the material and size were also different, so it was unlikely to mistake one for the other.

"Wait, this face…" Kaoru had a bad feeling about this.

"…They don't count currency by saying 'this many gold coins and this many silver coins' anymore, but by monetary units. Like yen or dollars. Though, I hear some people still count them the old-fashioned way. So, the unit they use for currency now…is called 'kaorun.' Named after the old saint, the Lady Angel…"

"Gyaaaaaa! I knew iiit!!!"

Sure enough, the face carved into the coin had quite a scary look in its eyes. Though, this was probably *after* they had made a bunch of adjustments, likely out of consideration for her image…

"W-Well, it isn't as if we can't use your old coins at all. I hear they're still accepted. It's a good thing that coins are valued based on the metals used instead of on a pure credit system. That said, they're worth about three percent less, so the shopkeeper might get annoyed trying to calculate their worth, and you'll stand out. It might be a good idea to find a place to exchange them as soon as possible…" Reiko said consolingly, but she knew that wasn't what Kaoru was shocked about. Unfortunately, there was nothing else she could really say in this situation…

It was still quite early when they secured their inn. Therefore, Kaoru couldn't let her day end already, having finally arrived in the royal capital. She and Reiko set out right away. Their destination was the house that Kaoru had bought for the orphans of the Eyes of the Goddess. Kaoru had read far too many stories where the character regretted putting off important things for later.

She didn't expect the house to still be there after over seventy years. And yet, she wanted to check to see if the building was still there now, then find out later whether the orphans were still alive. But…

"Why is it still there…? And it's still being used…" It would have been one thing if it had been built out of bricks, but it was an average house made of wood. She had originally rented it out, then purchased it later, but it was already quite old at that point. There was no way it could have been used for seventy more years. It wasn't as if it was made with particularly good materials and construction…

The house looked just as it did before… It obviously showed signs of wear, but it had been repaired and cared for. However, its surroundings had changed significantly.

Large shops stood on either side of the building, with several large multi-family dwellings behind it. Moreover, there were a variety of residences, ranging from what seemed to be dormitories for single workers to individual family homes.

"They must have preserved this place even as its surrounding land was developed and sold off… I told them to sell the house and split up the funds so they could go off into the world… Those idiots…"

Those kids must have married and had children and grandchildren since, with one of them living in the house so they could keep managing it, believing that Kaoru could return again some day…

Even though the chances of that happening were pretty much zero.

As Kaoru thought about it, she couldn't help hot tears from pouring down her cheeks.

"Huh? What the…"

Kaoru calmed down after some time, then noticed a sign next to the entrance of the building. She approached it and read the text…

"Chief Temple of the Order of the Goddess Kaoru."

"What the heck is thaaaaaat?!"

Reiko quickly covered Kaoru's mouth to stifle her outburst. Once she confirmed that her friend had settled down, she pointed at the signs at the shops on either side of the building.

The Eyes of the Goddess Apothecary

The Eyes of the Goddess Souvenir Store

"Get your Lady Kaoru rice crackers here!"

"They own all these shops?! And why rice crackers instead of manju?! Is it to spite me? Huh?!"

Chapter 46:
Long Goodbye

Afterward, Kaoru and Reiko quickly returned to their inn.

Kaoru had ended up getting a little too rowdy. People might have come out of their homes and shops to see what was going on if they had stayed any longer, so Reiko grabbed her by the arm to make a quick retreat.

Judging by the state of things, it would be easy enough to confirm if anyone was still alive, and it was unlikely that they were struggling to make ends meet. This gave Kaoru some peace of mind.

"You can make big money off religion, after all…" Reiko said bluntly.

She hadn't changed at all. What happened to the several decades' worth of life experience…? Such thoughts crossed Kaoru's mind as she hung her head.

The two rested at the inn for the evening and decided to proceed onward the next day.

When they got up the next morning, the two decided to go to the library instead of going straight to the Eyes of the Goddess headquarters. They decided it was smarter to get a better understanding of the situation before making their move.

The library was still in the same spot as before, and the entrance fee was still quite expensive. It cost the same number of silver coins, but perhaps that was because the monetary value had changed.

Of course, Kaoru and Reiko headed straight for the history books section. The first book Kaoru picked up was "The History of the Kingdom of Balmore." If you want to research a country, pick its official history.

It would obviously be somewhat skewed to make the royal family look good, but it was a far better option than a book written by some nobody with limited knowledge or biases, or a book written by some aristocrat to make their own house look like heroes.

And so, Kaoru read the history book.

She pretended not to see the books in the religion section, all with titles like, "All About the Order of the Goddess Kaoru," "A Goddess or an Angel? The Mystery of Lady Kaoru," "Famous Quotes by Lady Kaoru," "Lady Kaoru's 99 Secrets," "The Lady Kaoru Diet," and "Don't Do It! Lady Kaoru's Breast Augmentation."

…Especially that last one!

Reiko was also reading books to learn more about what was going on in this world. It was pointless for her to learn about things that had already happened, and she wasn't interested in reading about history that she'd had no part in making. It was far more useful for her to research matters of the present, especially considering she didn't know much about this world at all.

After learning about the events of around seventy years ago, Kaoru went around the various sections of the library to read a collection of significant incidents throughout history, mostly from publications akin to local newspapers, and various booklets written by people who were involved in events as they occurred.

Her own incident was quite a big deal, so there were many books related to it, but they were handwritten in ink with big letters and few pages, so she was able to get through them pretty quickly.

She ended up concentrating on her reading so hard that she found herself lost in the pages, and didn't notice the time until the librarian tapped her on the shoulder to let her know they were closing.

"All we managed to do today was read in the library... But I guess that's fine, considering it was something we needed to do anyway..." Kaoru said quietly.

"So, what did you find out?" Reiko asked, but judging by what they'd seen in the so-called Sacred Ground of Brancott's royal capital and her old home in this city, it was clear that Kaoru hadn't been made out as some villain. In fact, there was no way that was the case, judging by the unified currency and the designs on the coins.

Of course, Reiko had a good idea of the state of things already.

"Well, the thing is..." Kaoru began to explain.

After Kaoru had been dropped into the trap and retreated into the Item Box to escape the boulder, the Goddess Celestine had descended and furiously declared she intended to destroy the continent. But the guardian of the continent, the great hero Francette, had prevented this from happening. The Goddess Celestine had decreed that the rightful heir of the Kingdom of Brancott was to dispose of the culprits.

Afterward, Brancott's first prince and rightful ruler took the throne. The second prince, who had plotted to usurp the throne and murdered his own father, was beheaded, and his wife and children were sentenced to death to prevent any incidents in the future. Of course, the former bishops of Rueda, who had put the second prince up to it, along with the aristocrats and merchants who were involved, were all guilty of the same crime. They were also sentenced to death, and their houses were wiped out.

It was the perfect time to rid the country of its corruption, and the sentences were understandably harsh, as they were afraid of what might happen if they didn't carry out the Goddess Celestine's orders. Not even the punished parties complained about their punishment. Perhaps even the most wicked of people couldn't stand the thought of the entire continent being destroyed because of them.

The remaining former bishops, who had no political ambition and fled from Rueda with their fortune to live in leisure, ended up getting the short end of the stick. The Goddess Celestine's orders spread out to the countries of the peninsulas as well, and each of them frantically searched for the former bishops, captured them, then sent their seized assets back to the Rueda region in the Kingdom of Balmore. This involved the lives of everyone on the continent, including themselves, after all.

There was a ghastly air about the search parties that had gone out to find the targets. And considering everyone on the entire continent was cooperating in the search, the former bishops who had been lax about protecting and managing their personal information were caught one by one.

However, it wasn't as if every one of them were put to death. Those who were unrelated to the incident and not corrupt managed to get away with just getting their funds confiscated.

Then, the first prince and newly crowned king of Brancott negotiated a peace treaty with the Kingdom of Balmore, along with a commercial treaty between the Kingdoms of Balmore, Brancott, Aseed, and the Aligot Empire. He also reached out to Brancott's neighbors, Drisard and the Kingdom of Jusral, and established a foundation for a common trading area among the peninsulas and their proximal countries.

"I had no idea that stalker was such a skilled politician... I'm impressed..." Kaoru said with a rather conflicted look, but this was all ultimately the result of Fernand being acknowledged as someone who Lady Kaoru the Angel had assisted because she deemed him worthy of the throne. Otherwise, he would have been dismissed as the useless youngster who had thrown the kingdom into chaos over his struggle for succession and failed to unify the various countries.

As for Francette, not only was she the hero who had saved the Kingdom of Balmore from the Aligot Empire's invasion, but she was now known for saving the continent from the evil clutches of the Goddess Celestine. The people treated the so-called guardian of the continent, the great hero Francette, as something akin to a living deity.

Her title was even upgraded two ranks to that of a marquess...

"'Evil clutches' of the Goddess, huh..." Reiko said flatly, but Kaoru just shrugged.

Francette and Roland's massive marriage ceremony was celebrated not only throughout Balmore, but in various other countries on the continent. They had a daughter together, who in turn married the crown prince — in other words, Roland's younger brother and King Serge's first son. Serge had cried tears of joy, stating that his older brother's bloodline had finally returned to the main royal line.

There wasn't much to be found about the Eyes of the Goddess. They were just a group of orphans who were taken care of by Kaoru, after all, so they must have been deemed too unimportant to be written about. Or perhaps the writers didn't want to record the fact that orphans were the closest to Kaoru, rather than the royal family, aristocrats, or priests. Such people were quite common, after all.

Still, the Order of the Goddess Kaoru was mentioned in several books.

The mainstream religion known as the Orthodox Order of the Goddess taught that Celestine was the one and only Goddess and that Kaoru was a human who had received her blessing. Meanwhile, the Order of the Goddess Kaoru was a smaller religion that taught that Kaoru was a friend of the Goddess Celestine and was a goddess herself, though it was treated as heresy by some.

Its founder's name was Emile Nagase.

"Huh? Is that your kid? And are you an aristocrat?"

"I'm still single, and I have ancient and honorable origins as a commoner! Emile is an orphan who lived with me," Kaoru replied as she scratched the tip of her nose.

"But you said only aristocrats have family names…"

"Usually, yeah, but some people like big-time merchants were allowed to call themselves by their family name or shop name, and these kids, uh…they asked me to adopt them. No girl could refuse a request like that with fourteen innocent eyes staring at them… So, I couldn't help but agree.

"Then they went on to say, 'All right, now we're Lady Kaoru's kin. We're her messengers, her tribe, her relatives, and her vassals… In other words, we're family!' Everyone knew I lived with those kids, which is probably why no one stopped them from using my family name. They were probably too afraid of angering Celes by saying something they weren't supposed to…"

"Ah… I guess most people would just look the other way, then. Those kids probably did that because they wanted you to be known by your proper, full name."

"Yeah…"

Knowing how Emile and the others felt, Kaoru had no intention of complaining about it.

"But I'm surprised they challenged the one and only religion by making their own, and they managed to survive until now. I thought the church had tremendous power in this world…"

"Temple, not church. Normally, you'd be right, but…"

103

Representative Follower: Francette Balmore.

Head Follower: Roland Balmore.

Main Followers: The Eyes of the Goddess, the House of Adan.

Foreign Branches: Beliscas — Centered around the House of Raphael and the House of Dorivell; Aligot Empire — Centered around the navy and associates of shipping companies.

"Yeah, no one's messing with a lineup like that..."

"Nope..."

After all, the guardian of the continent, the great hero Francette and her husband, the brother of the king himself, were the principal organizers. Not to mention, they had expanded into the militaries of friendly countries. If they tried to persecute them... No, more importantly, they could have angered the Goddess Celestine.

"Oh, I guess Mariel's house had their title upgraded... And that boy's house had a baronial title before..." Indeed, they had respectively been upgraded from viscount to count, and from baron to viscount. The reason wasn't stated in the records.

"Well, I guess there's no reason to write about aristocrats from other countries," Kaoru said and brushed it off. She didn't even consider that there may have been a reason why they *couldn't* write about it in their text...

"So, as far as I could tell from those books, those kids lived relatively normal lives beside the whole starting a weird religion thing, and managed not to get dragged into any conflict that would be in the records. I guess they did pretty well for themselves if they lived normal, happy lives as orphans..."

"...Don't you think to yourself, 'What if I could have given them even better lives?'"

"Huh?" Kaoru cocked her head and looked at Reiko blankly.

She didn't really understand what her friend was saying. There was no point in thinking that way, and it would only do more harm than good now. But...

"What if you could go back in time?"

"What...?" Kaoru froze. She loved reading, too. She had read tons of short stories involving time travel and time machines, along with manga, anime, and movies.

"...You can do that?"

"I haven't tried, but probably not. That sounds like something that would conflict with the Goddess's job of stopping this dimension from crumbling. Like, if we caused a divergence by going back through time or something..."

"Ahh, right..."

It seemed Reiko simply wanted to know how Kaoru felt... Or perhaps she suspected her friend could be thinking that she could have given those kids happier lives if she had taken better care of them, and wanted her to say it out loud rather than internally torture herself over the thought.

"...But even if that was possible... I'd pass. If I could go back in time and fix things, all the things that happened to the people of this world over the past seventy years... Their efforts and their results, the fulfilled and unfilled dreams, the people who were born... Not even a god could just wipe all that away as if it never happened.

"And even if I could redo the mistakes of my past, it's highly likely that it would just create a new world that had diverged from this one, and this one would go on after you and I disappeared from it. Nothing would change in this world if that happened, so it'd be pointless.

"Meanwhile, I'm supposed to take on the responsibility for all the lives and their misfortunes and tragedies in this new world? No thanks! I'll leave that up to the gods. It's too heavy for me!"

Kaoru had no intention of taking on such a burden. You only had one shot at life, after all, and there was no starting over or shuffling for a new hand. You had to play the hand you were dealt. It didn't matter if you got a full house or some random junk.

Kaoru mulled over such thoughts, then...

"Oh, wait, I actually did get to reset my life..."

"I'm replaying mine too, I guess," Reiko replied.

The two laughed awkwardly.

"Well, I figured you'd say that, Kaoru. I don't even know if it's possible to go back in the first place..."

"Yeah. That's one line humans shouldn't cross..."

It seemed Reiko asked her the question knowing that Kaoru wouldn't want to do such a thing. She had said it so her friend could say it out loud and have closure rather than just mulling it over in her head. And of course, Kaoru understood this as well.

"...You really are Reiko, Reiko."

"What are you going on about now...?"

The next morning...

It was time for Kaoru to check and see how her old acquaintances were doing. However, considering how short the average lifespan was in this world, it was unlikely that many of them were still alive.

Kaoru had been reincarnated in her fifteen-year-old body, and it had been a little less than five years since then. She was just under twenty years old when she vanished, so anyone older than her at that point would be over ninety now.

...Her hope was slim. Even among the orphans, Emile had been sixteen, Belle twelve, and Layette six at the time. They would all be around eighty or older now. It was pretty rough.

But at least Kaoru could find out if they'd had children or grandchildren, and find whatever mark they had left in the world. After all, they had started up some shops owned by a religious sect, and those were pretty hard to miss.

"Hair and eye color change, check! Makeup that makes the sides of my eyes droop downward, check! Money I borrowed from Reiko, check! Time to go!"

Their first destination was that shop. A customer would naturally walk into a business establishment, after all. There was absolutely nothing out of the ordinary about that. And as a traveler from far away, there was nothing suspicious about me asking a bunch of questions of whoever worked there. It was the perfect cover for gathering intel.

And so...

"I'm going in!"

"R-Right..."

Kaoru made her declaration after deliberating about it in front of the store entrance for some time, and Reiko nodded in turn. The door swung open, and the two entered the shop. They had decided to go into the apothecary rather than the souvenir store. Kaoru figured there would be fewer customers there, giving her more time to chat with the employee.

As the two entered, someone welcomed them from behind the counter. The attendant was about sixty or so, which was pretty old in this world. Well, a souvenir shop was one thing, but a young shop attendant wouldn't have been a good fit for this type of store. It was pretty much a rule that apothecaries had to be run by old people.

Now, I need to come up with an opener that will make me look like a customer willing to pay, but it has to be a topic that won't just end with me buying the product... Yes, I need to talk about something expensive that only a specialist would know and is probably unavailable here, then expand on the discussion from there... I know just the thing!

"Do you have hemort seeds, mortgul fruits, and kurcul leaves in stock?"

Indeed, those were the ultra-rare and expensive ingredients for Longevity Medicine. Asking for those ingredients indicated that she knew about Longevity Medicine and its ingredients, and that she wasn't just an average commoner. This would prove Kaoru and Reiko were extraordinary visitors, and set her up to discuss how to obtain expensive ingredients that were unavailable here, as well as other topics. But...

"Yes, we do. The portions needed to make a bottle of Longevity Medicine will be thirty-five gold coins total. We can mix them here, too."

"You do?!" Kaoru exclaimed.

I had tried to make the apothecary attendant think I was someone special by bluffing with the medicinal knowledge I had gained from that previous incident. I thought I could accomplish this by mentioning the base ingredients for Longevity Medicine, which were rare and expensive, and few knew how to mix it correctly.

But it turned out...they had them ALL in stock!

Haah... Haah...

Well, come to think of it, over seventy years have passed since then. Maybe technology has advanced and they can now harvest rare herbs, like what happened to Asian ginseng in Japan.

...I messed up.

There had been a drastic change in the seventy years between the Showa to Heisei eras, but changes over seventy years in the older eras were negligible. That's why I had assumed civilization hadn't changed much over that span in this world. And yet...

No, but if that was the case, it was strange that the price he quoted hadn't changed much from what it was in the past. That meant the value of the medicine and its ingredients were the same as back then...

Either this shop was unusually well-stocked, this just happened to be the season when these three items were harvested, or Longevity Medicine had become wildly popular since the disappearance of my potions...

In any case, this shop had the three main ingredients for Longevity Medicine, its price was still stupid high, and I had asked if they had it in stock...

But I only asked if they have it in stock and haven't said I'll buy it yet! We're good! We're good!!! Haah... Haah...

"..." The aged shopkeeper stared at me dubiously as I stood there silently.

"..."

Awkward...

"..."

Ahhhhhh!

"...Well, it is quite a pricey item, and I understand if you don't want to reveal that you need it. Let us talk in the back for a bit. Someone watch the counter for me!"

Ahhh, I don't like where this is going! ...Well, I guess I'll just get some info out of him in the back and get out after buying some less expensive medicine.

Medicine... It had to be the least convenient item for me... I would've been better off with some rice crackers from the souvenir shop!

And so, I was led into a small room in the back, where a female employee laid out some tea and snacks, then retreated.

"...So, what's the meaning of this?"

Huh? Is he mad at me? He seems really upset...

Maybe he was angry because I asked about an expensive item I had no intention of buying. But, I mean, wasn't it normal for someone to hesitate before making a big purchase? It seemed odd that an aged and experienced shopkeeper would get so emotional over something like this. Maybe things were just different here compared to Japan...

"I said, what's the meaning of this?! Why... Why did you take so long, Lady Kaoru... U-Uu... Uaaaaaah!!!"

The old man leaped forward and embraced me while bawling his eyes out, and I just stood there, dumbfounded and unable to even push him away.

Then a realization came to me, and I asked in a near whisper, "...E...mile...?" It felt like there was a shadow of that young boy's familiar face when I looked at him. Well, I say familiar, but it had been only a few days from my perspective...

But...

"Sorry... I'm sorry..."

All I could do was apologize, and all I could do was cry. It may have been just a brief moment for me, but it must have been an unfathomably long time for them. A whole lifetime.

He spent his whole life waiting for me...

"Well, I did get married to Belle and had children — down to great-great-grandchildren — made a killing with my business, and lived a life of comfort," he added.

"Whaaaaaat?!"

After finally calming down, the old man — Emile, rather — explained what had happened after the incident.

With Emile, I knew I could ask anything without holding back, and he was likely to know pretty much everything I wanted to find out. The Emile I had known wouldn't have sat idly by without investigating every detail of what had happened. He'd had plenty of time, after all. Over seventy years, in fact...

Oh, and although he complained about me showing up so late, I told him it had been only a few days for me, and he backed off after that. That was the truth, after all.

I heard Emile muttering to himself, "Damn, does time flow at a different rate in the realm of gods compared to our world? Or maybe they perceive time differently after living for tens of thousands of years...?" but he seemed to understand. Mhm.

And so...

"What? Seven of the original members of the Eyes of the Goddess, including Belle, are still alive? Layette and Francette, too?"

"Yes. Wally died in a carriage accident, and Ike was attacked by bandits on the way back from stocking up on goods... Everyone else is doing well. We used the you-know-what whenever there was a lethal epidemic or a serious injury..."

Ah... They must have used the three dozen all-purpose special potions, the ones with no expiration date, that were hidden under the floorboards. They must have used them to recover from illnesses and injuries that they wouldn't have survived otherwise...

Of course they wouldn't die so easily, unless they had died instantly or perished before they could make it here.

"But you were the oldest of the Eyes of the Goddess, Emile. Aren't you like ninety now? You don't look any older than sixty…"

Emile did look incredibly young for his age. That was why I hadn't noticed who he was at all at first. I may have noticed something if he had been a decrepit old man who looked like he would fall over any minute.

"Yeah, we're all really lively. Our medicine has a reputation for being effective and blessed by the Goddess, which is one of the reasons our business has been going so well. And we hardly ever get sick, either. Though, even we get sick during major plagues or anything like that…"

Emile still talked like a youngster despite his age. He probably talked more maturely in his everyday life, but was talking to me like he used to. I figured he didn't want to act differently with me. It probably felt as if we had gone back in time to the good old days.

"Ah."

Then, I realized something. The reason Emile and the others were so youthful and resistant to disease was probably because of my potions. When I first met them, they had accumulated a bunch of little injuries and illnesses, and were skin and bones from malnutrition, so I had given them potions that would completely heal them. Unlike the potions I made with limited functionality later on, I hadn't put much thought into those.

Potions that completely cured illnesses… This meant they affected illnesses embedded in their genetics that could have manifested later on, DNA transcription errors, and the repairing of shortened telomeres, so it messed with all sorts of stuff…

It was no wonder people assumed they were blessed by Celes and didn't want to mess with them... That explained why their business thrived without them being harassed by those in power, local thugs, or competitors.

Hey, that's cheating!!!

"So, has Layette been with you guys, too?"

"Yeah. The seven of us started a business with that house as our headquarters. We ran the business from the house instead of going out to work, because it was much safer and we could all be together. It was more convenient for us to protect the house and the you-know-what as long as we were there, too.

"Owning a house meant we didn't need to pay rent for our home or shop, and we had seven workers willing to work for free, so we made money for food and necessities pretty easily. Besides, there was no way we weren't gonna get customers when we were the children Lady Kaoru had taken care of, living in Lady Kaoru's former home."

"That's cheating!"

It was no wonder they were able to make money.

...Wait, seven? Wouldn't it be eight, including Layette...? Oh, Lolotte must have moved out to be with Achille.

"The first product we started handling was, of course, apothecary related. Our shop was the Angel's, after all. Since we didn't want people to expect our goods to be as effective as your potions, we only sold the ingredients instead of the medicine itself. It wasn't as if we had the necessary knowledge, skills, or credentials to even make our own medicine, after all. Oh, but these days we do have skilled staff, so we mix it in-house now. I've also become accredited, myself."

Emile had dedicated himself to training in swordsmanship, but he'd done it so he could keep me safe. After I had disappeared and he lost the ability to move how he used to, he had his willing descendants take up martial arts so they could be appointed as my bodyguards if I ever returned.

And so, he had taken up handling the desk work. Emile never did like violence or hurting others, after all. He didn't hate sword training, considering he was doing it so he could protect me, but it likely wasn't the path he truly wanted to take. With my disappearance and him in his old age, he was finally released from the duty that had bound him...

Maybe if I had never met him, he could have taken the path he wanted to from the start... Nah. It was likely that he would never have gotten himself a proper job, and as an orphan, he probably would've ended up dead with his head in the gutter somewhere. He did more than well for himself simply by living to this age. So, there was no need for me to feel responsible. Not in the slightest.

...But still... I couldn't just compartmentalize it like that.

"Lolotte was taken in by Fran as her foster daughter and married Achille to become his lawful wife as a marquise's daughter. This was before Fran married Roland, so she was still a marquise. Achille became a baron, but although Lolotte was just a foster daughter, she was the foster daughter of the guardian of the continent, the great hero Francette. Not to mention, she was the lawful wife of a duke, and one who was soon to be the brother of His Majesty the King at that. She could have married into the royal family if she wanted..."

He did have a point...

"So, Fran rose up two whole ranks, huh? A commoner suddenly jumped up to a viscountess, then a marquise..." I noted.

"Look, she earned the title of viscountess after saving the kingdom and being lauded as a great hero. It's more surprising that an aristocrat who saved every living being in the land, the one who became the guardian of the continent, only had their title increased by two ranks! Though, I guess it wouldn't have been easy to make her a duchess."

Yup, pretty much only the royals could earn that title. Besides, she was going to be married to a duke soon after, so it probably didn't matter much. Francette herself didn't seem to care too much about such things, anyway.

"At the time, Fran also asked Layette if she wanted to become her foster daughter too, but Layette refused and said, 'The only family name I will go by is Nagase!' Though, Lolotte still calls herself Lolotte Nagase von Lolotte, and she stops by here pretty often... I remember Achille complaining about it all the time when they were newlyweds."

I couldn't blame him...

"Everyone's pretty free these days, so we've been meeting up once a week without fail," Emile said.

"Hm? What about Achille?"

"...How old do you think he'd be if he was still alive? And do you know the average lifespan of men in this country?"

" ..."

...Right. Achille never had one of my super potions, and I had forbidden the children from giving them to anyone who wasn't a member of the Eyes of the Goddess or telling anyone else about their existence. It was very unlikely for them to disobey a direct order like that from me, even if their lives were under threat.

"Fran is still alive and kicking, of course. As long as she's around, no kingdom dares oppose ours. Some people don't like her because of how serious she is, but this is the great hero Fran we're talking about..."

"Yeah... No one would wanna go against her..."

I felt bad for the royal family...

About Fran saving the continent…it wasn't as if she had fought her way through the enemy ranks and defeated a demon lord or something, but it was true that the entire land would have been drowned underwater if she hadn't mustered the courage to talk back to Celes.

In a sense, Fran was indeed a true hero and had definitely saved the continent from the demon lord (Celes).

"What about Ed and the others?" I asked.

"We didn't have the money to take care of horses at the time, so Fran took in all three of them. She looked after them along with her and Roland's horses, but all five of the horses had an abnormal amount of stamina, so they were treated well as the divine horses who had served the Angel, and lived long lives as breeding horses. Those five left a bunch of descendants, which are generally known as Silvers. They're pretty much a brand name these days."

Ah…

Yeah, I knew this might happen. I had given them a bunch of potions in the past, but seventy years was too long for a horse to live. But if he lived a long life and left a bunch of offspring, I guess he got what they wanted as animals… Wait, did I really lose to a horse?! And if he was a breeding horse, that means he was a stud, right? Was he cheating, then? He had a wife and daughter… Though, I guess human logic didn't really apply to animals.

It wasn't uncommon for human men to have multiple wives, even in certain countries on Earth to this day. Not to mention, it was incredibly hard for a female to give birth to a hundred children, but it wasn't impossible for a male to have a hundred kids.

In fact, there's a man named Mitsumasa Kido who fathered a hundred boys… Wait, that was from a manga, so I guess that didn't count.

But…

"Ed never found out why I didn't come back, huh... He probably thought I died..."

"Oh, no, Ed and the others knew everything," Emile replied.

"Huh?"

"About two months after the incident, a female aristocrat arrived from a distant country. She explained everything to Ed and the others after looking into the facts. Your body hadn't been found, even after the boulder was moved, so she said that you erased the damaged physical form that you'd taken on in this world and returned to your own."

"What? You mean..."

A female aristocrat who could talk to Ed besides me...

"Yeah, it was Countess Raphael of the Order of the Goddess Kaoru's Beliscas branch. Though, she was still a viscountess at the time. She claimed only she could explain the situation to Ed, brushed the aristocrats and royal family aside as they tried to stop her, and showed up with Carlos. She said it was because she owed a great debt to Ed..."

I see...

Mariel came all this way for Ed... Giving Mariel a potion that allowed her to communicate with animals wasn't a waste after all...

I had found out everything I wanted to know. It seemed everyone lived relatively fruitful and happy lives. There was no need for me anymore. It was time for us to depart on our journey. A journey for two with just me and Reiko. We were always a trio along with Kyoko, so it felt kind of fresh with just us two.

And so...

"Sorry for the wait, Reiko. Let's get going, then!"

"Right," Reiko replied.

"…Wait! Wait, wait, wait, wait, waaaiiit! I'll be killed if I let you leave now! By Belle and Layette, especially!"

Not my problem…

"No, it's better for me to leave like this. Everyone's living good lives now. If I showed up suddenly, they'd all be bound by their pasts again. Besides, I want to remember everyone the way I knew them back then…"

"…"

There must have been a lot he wanted to say, but Emile just hung his head in silence in response. With his unnaturally youthful appearance compared to his peers, and having lived far longer than the average lifespan of this world, Emile must have understood the pain of not aging or dying, and the sorrow of seeing others pass away around him. Knowing that we couldn't spend time together as we once had even if we were to reunite, it was better to confirm that everyone was still doing well, and to remember them the way they were during our happiest times together.

Emile must have understood how I felt. He had to. He was nearly ninety years old himself. He must have seen many people die before him. Close friends, others who weren't so close… So many people… Emile still had Belle and his friends from the Eyes of the Goddess, those who had walked the same path as him. But if he had been all alone…

"…Okay. You're a goddess, and it's not as if I never considered that you staying with us humans for so long could go against the ways of the gods. I have had plenty of time to think, after all… So I think you should do as you please. We had no right to bind you in the first place, nor do we want to.

"I just want you to do what you want and enjoy what this world has to offer. That's why you took some time off from your duties as

119

a goddess and came to visit this world run by your friend, the Goddess Celestine, right? And if there are people you happen to save along the way... I mean, you've already saved us. So there's no need for you to stay here any longer. But..."

"But?"

"When the others find out I got to talk to you, they're gonna beat me half to death...or kill me outright! So, please, leave me a potion! I can't use the ones we keep underground for something like this..."

Ah... Those must have been treasures for the Eyes of the Goddess. Not for how effective they were, but because they were gifts from me. He couldn't just use one for something like this. There must have been so many times when they had thought about using a potion but refrained. Those potions wouldn't still be here otherwise. But if they did kill Emile outright, he'd perish before being able to drink my potion...

So...

And...there.

"If you feel like you're in danger, drink this. This potion will heal your wounds for some time after you drink it."

"Thank you!!!" Emile tucked the potion bottle into his pocket with a gleeful expression.

...There was something I didn't realize at the time. I didn't imagine what the others, especially Belle, Layette, and Francette, would do — with terrifying smiles on their faces — when they realized Emile would heal immediately even when they punished him. He'd be the traitor who had gotten to talk to Lady Kaoru by himself and even received a gift from her, after all. Of course things would escalate if he recovered after getting beaten up...

"Anyway, farewell!" I said, and as I turned to leave...

"…Well, even if I suddenly drop dead, I lived a good life already. And I think it's about time I passed my authority on to the younger generation… Maybe I'll retire and become the keeper of the Order of the Goddess Kaoru Head Temple or something…" Emile muttered to himself.

The "Head Temple" was probably the house I had given them. Well, he was already pretty old, so maybe living a quiet life in retirement wasn't a bad idea.

…*Ah.*

"Hey, is the Order of the Goddess Kaoru in opposition with the Orthodox Order of the Goddess? Have there been any troubles between the two? I couldn't find any specifics on sensitive topics like that in any books at the library…"

I had to find out about this, or I might accidentally let slip a no-no word and unintentionally cause problems. It was common knowledge that talking about curry, ramen, your favorite baseball team, politics, and religion was asking for trouble. …Though, those first three didn't exist in this world.

"Nope," Emile replied.

…It was that simple?

"The Order of the Goddess Kaoru is considered to be a sect that branched off from Lady Celestine's Orthodox Order of the Goddess. The Orthodox Order of the Goddess considers you a saint, known as the Angel, but still an ordinary human who was blessed by the Goddess Celestine. Meanwhile, we treat you as a goddess who is on the same level as the Goddess Celestine. Both orders worship you and the Goddess Celestine, so we're the same in that sense. When you became a martyr and ascended to the heavens, even the Orthodox Order of the Goddess started treating you with reverence at a level just below Lady Celestine."

That sounded kinda like two religions back on Earth...

"Besides, we don't try to spread our religion. It's just us, who were directly helped by you, and those who know that you're a goddess, doing this on our own. That's because we couldn't accept that you were just a human that was a sort of messenger for the Goddess Celestine. Besides, it's not like anyone can try to mess with us when Fran, Roland, and other powerful people are involved. We aren't trying to expand our influence or threaten other religions... Whatever earnings we make are just from genuine business activity. I mean, we did get a huge boost from using your name, but making money was pretty easy when we used what you taught us about economics and running businesses..."

...

......

....

Th-These kids...

They grew up so strong...

There really was nothing left for me to do here.

...Wait, what can a little brat like me be able to do for a nearly ninety-year-old senior?!

It was time to say goodbye for real this time.

"Hey, on second thought, maybe just once... Maybe you could join us for dinner tonight, together..." Emile said, still unable to give up on the idea, but...

I shook my head in silence. I guess this was our very own *The Long Goodbye*. The title sounded pretty lame in Japanese. It was a shame, because the translated title for *Farewell, My Lovely* was wonderful...

In any case, it was time to depart gracefully.

"Oh, wait a second!" Emile stopped me once again.

"Here, take this as a souvenir. It's our specialty, a Lady Kaoru Rice Cracker. We designed it based on our collective memories. We're pretty proud of it!"

"Why is it a rice cracker instead of manju?! Are you saying my form can be replicated on a completely flat surface?!"

I have some curves too, damn it!!!

"Kaoru, how much longer are we delaying this...?" Reiko said in an exasperated tone from beside me.

Shaddap!

Chapter 47:
New Departure

It had dragged on for a pretty long time, but it was finally time for us to be on our way! Emile asked to see my real face one last time, so I changed my hair and eye colors back to normal and took off the clear tape on my eyes.

Over seventy years had passed since my disappearance, so it was unlikely that anyone would recognize my face other than people who had been close to me. ...Honestly, it was unlikely that those people would be alive at all, let alone remember me.

There may have been pictures of me still around, but it wasn't as if they were portraits drawn by professionals. They were based on memory, which was prone to being idealized or deformed. Just like the too-beautiful version of my face engraved in the currency here...

Besides, everyone other than those close to me thought I was just an ordinary human that had been liked by Celes, so no one expected me to look exactly the same as back then. They probably thought I had ascended to the heavens at the time anyway...

So, there was no need to wear a disguise anymore.

I originally disguised myself in case those close to me were still alive, but they could recognize me anyway, so there was no point... Also, the pieces of tape on the sides of my eyes were pulling at my face and it was really annoying.

After talking with Emile to his heart's content, it was time to go for real. We left the apothecary, and as we passed by the Head Temple...

There!

Yup, I knew they wouldn't have gotten rid of the secret container I had made and put under the floorboards. That's why I figured the non-expiring special potions were still hidden in the same spot.

So, okay, I added some extra potions there for them. Their bodies were probably reaching their limits soon. I wanted them to drink the potions and avoid suffering through calculi or things like that. …I could even make potions that would make them younger. What if I gave some to Emile and the others? …No, that wasn't it.

That was something I wasn't supposed to do. It wouldn't have been good for me…or for them. Besides, those in power wouldn't just sit idly by if they found out about this. They would come after Emile and the others in full force.

…Immortality would only bring disaster.

Emile would be telling the others about me after dinner, so I still had time to get out of the city. I had visited the shop first thing in the morning, so I was in no rush.

And so, I passed through the central plaza and went by the Temple of the Goddess and toward the suburbs. I headed east from there. To the west were some mountain ranges, the Aligot Empire, and the sea. To the north was the sea. To the south was the Kingdom of Aseed…and the sea.

Yup, east was my only choice here. I mean, now that the Aligot Empire was a maritime power, a voyage by sea using one of their ships wasn't out of the question. But it sounded like a hassle, and traveling to some distant country didn't sound all too charming to me.

And a part of me wanted to go back along routes I had taken in the past to see how they looked now. Slow and steady was the key here… I had time, after all. More than enough time. Reiko and I both.

"Take it easy!" as they say...

A journey with the two of us... We could travel light, since I had my Item Box, and we didn't really need water with my ability to make potions. We could walk, but our pace was about seventy percent of a normal traveler's. That sounded tiring, too...

Even if I could heal myself with potions, it wasn't as if I enjoyed getting blisters on my feet. But if we decided to ride on stagecoaches, we would only be able to travel during their operating hours, and our topics of conversation weren't really appropriate in front of others.

It would be bad if we talked about taboo stuff in the language of this world, but speaking in a foreign language was even worse. It would draw suspicion, and speaking in a language that only we understood would make it look like we were discussing secrets. Anyway, it wasn't good manners.

Besides, we wouldn't be able to cook with food in my Item Box or use the shower room with a tank filled with rinsing potion attached if we traveled with others. A long journey under those conditions would be a bit difficult for someone who was used to modern comforts.

So...

As I contemplated this while we walked, Reiko suddenly stopped in her tracks, and I stopped too.

...

......

....

"Kaoru, don't tell me..."

Don't say it.

"Is this..." she went on.

Don't say it...

Yes, it was the giant Celes statue near the entrance of the Temple of the Goddess that we had seen long ago. Next to it was a statue of a valiant female knight. It went without saying that it was a statue of the great hero who saved the kingdom — no, the entire continent.

And on the other side of it was a statue of a girl with scary-looking eyes.

"A statue of…" Reiko continued.

"Don't say iiiiiit!!!"

Judging by the composition of the statues, it seemed Fran was venerated above me. I guess that was to be expected. It was between a commoner girl who was kind of liked by the Goddess and who died pointlessly, and the savior and guardian of the entire continent, the great hero who happened to be a high-ranking aristocrat and wife of the king's brother. Of course they would treat her differently.

I mean, I was glad Celes's and Fran's statues drew attention away from mine, so I had no intention of complaining.

…We pressed forward without saying anything.

After walking for some time…

"Oh, this place…" I said.

"What is it?"

"Oh, it's just that this is the horse stable where I left Ed…my horse partner and brother-in-arms…along with his wife and child. It's been so long since, but it hasn't changed a bit…"

Although over seventy years had passed, it felt like just a few days ago to me. The memory was still fresh in my mind. It was incredible to think it looked pretty much the same after all this time… oh, but the main building looked like it had been rebuilt. And…wait, I thought that was a horse, but maybe it was a statue of some sort?

"Mind if I stop by here for a bit?"

"We have time, so why not?"

With Reiko's agreement, I moved closer to what seemed to be a bronze statue…

"…Ed? And his family…?"

Indeed, there stood a life-sized statue of Ed and his wife and child. Francette and Roland's horses weren't there, likely because those two were unrelated to these stables. It could be said that Ed's family was from these stables, so they seemed to be using that fact for marketing purposes…

Horses looked pretty much alike, and Ed had been a white horse with no distinct features on his body. Seeing him in the flesh was one thing, but it was hard to tell him apart from other horses just from a picture or statue.

But that didn't matter. It was Ed. I knew it was a statue of Ed. There was no mistake.

…Because…it's Ed…

I stood there feeling sentimental, then a white horse that looked a bit like Ed came closer.

Then…

"Can it be… Goddess Kaoru…?"

"Huh? You know me?"

I was surprised. How did a horse I had just met for the first time know me?

"You are?" I asked.

"Ah! You can understand me! Ah! Ah! Ahhh! I knew it! You must be the Goddess Lady Kaoru, benefactor of the first Silver horse, Ed Silver!"

The horse was so emotional that his body trembled with excitement. It seemed he was Ed's descendant. I had no idea horses had the intellect or culture to pass down stories about me over generations…

"I am 'Hanging Eyes,' also known as Hang, he who was appointed the twelfth-generation Ed Silver. It's a pleasure to meet you."

"Ed Silver is a title...? And that name sounds like a jab at me, somehow..."

"Oh, goodness, no! 'Hanging Eyes' is not just my given name, but a prestigious ancestral inheritance, given by the first generation Ed Silver to his son to remind him of you, Lady Kaoru!"

Ah... Ed probably just had trouble coming up with other words to describe me. Horses didn't exactly have the greatest vocabularies, after all...

...Damn it!

Well, assuming they had a foal at around six years old, twelve generations of horses would be seventy-two years. The math checked out...

"Hey, what are you doing, Hang?"

Ah, another horse was approaching...

"Ohh! Lady Kaoru, this one here is another who has inherited one of the prestigious names passed down from our ancestors: 'Scary Eyes.' He and I will carry on the Eyes Clan together!"

"I figured he'd have a name like that!" I shouted.

Damn it!

"Within the Silver breed, there's also 'Flat Chest' and 'No Chest' of the distinguished Chest Clan, along with those of the Breast Clan..."

"Shaddap!!!"

Damn that Ed! He definitely assumed I left him behind and did this to spite me! At least only the horses called each other by those names...

"Lady Kaoru is here?! Then does that mean the glory days of the Silver breed will return once again? And the time has come during our age of the Eyes Clan... The golden age... I can see it now... Ahh! Ahh! Ahhh!"

What was all this now...?

"Actually, I just happened to stop by because this place made me feel nostalgic. I'm glad to see Ed's descendants flourishing. Though, I feel like they might have flourished a bit too much..."

I've heard that, back on Earth, the paternal lines of all thoroughbred horses in modern times could be traced back to three horses. It seemed that Ed had become the ancestor of every one of these so-called Silver horses.

...I'm so jealous...

Damn it!!!

"Well, I'll be going. Farewell, everyone!"

As I turned to leave...

"Wait! Please wait!"

"No! Don't let her escape! Seize her! Seize her, boys!"

Two of the horses suddenly shouted out, then all of the grazing horses came rushing toward me at once.

...This is freaking me out here!

The next moment, we found ourselves surrounded.

"I will accompany you!"

Huh?

"In his last words, the first Ed Silver once told me that if the Goddess Lady Kaoru ever descended again..."

What...? Ed left his last words to his descendants to support me in his stead...? He really did care...

"He said I'll be set for life if I followed you, so I should never let you go!" the horse finished.

Yeah, I figured as much…

"So, please allow me to accompany you!"

"And me too, of course! As the horse who inherited the name of Scary Eyes, I'm a member of this ranch's Eyes Clan, just like Hanging Eyes! I ain't letting you leave me behind! There are two of you, anyway, so you've got no reason to refuse!"

Uhh…

"If you aren't willing to take us…"

"Then what?" I asked.

"Then we'll kill ourselves right nooow!" they yelled together.

Ah… Well, it wasn't as if I didn't understand how they felt. I had shown up, just like in the stories passed down by the First (Ed), so ancestral shame would haunt them forever if I just ignored them and left.

I glanced over at Reiko…

And she nodded. She had the ability to understand any language and conversation like me, so she had been following along the entire time.

"I'm prepared for that, of course. I've gone to riding clubs, ridden on horses without saddles, and I even participated in a few rough stock events."

Ah… I had to admit, long journeys on foot were pretty rough, too… If we were gonna get horses anyway, I'd rather go with Ed's descendants rather than some horses I didn't know. But weren't these the two best horses at the ranch? They would probably cost me an arm and a leg…

Oh well. In my past life…no, last time…well, that didn't feel quite right either. In the first season…I had saved up a boatload of gold coins in my Item Box, so I wasn't too concerned about the price.

All right!

"You two don't have any qualms about pulling a carriage, do you?" I asked.

"Ah, you speak of the Goddess's legendary Chariot that can only be pulled by divine horses! What an honor this is!" Hang said.

"Yes! Yes, I'll pull it! I'll pull it even if you tell me not to! Let's gooo!!!" Scary agreed.

So it was decided…

"I'm gonna go negotiate, then, so you stay here."

"We'll accompany you!"

We would be speaking in human language, so it wasn't as if they'd be able to understand us… But I didn't mind.

"So, I'd like for you to sell me these two horses…"

"What do you mean, 'so'?! And these are my two best horses!"

Yes, I would have had a hard time getting to the negotiation part if he didn't know which horses I was talking about, so I let the two of them follow me to the administrative building. And when I opened the door and stepped inside, the horses followed. The entrance was pretty small for a horse, but they forced their way in anyway… It was no wonder the manager came running out to see what was going on…

And so, here we were.

"No, no, no! I can't agree to that, even if you weren't just a kid yanking my chain. These two have the most of their ancestor's blood, making them extremely valuable. I need them to impreg…make a bunch of babies for me, so the answer is no, no matter how much you offer!"

He seemed to reconsider using such graphic words to a child and corrected himself mid-sentence. Not to mention, he took the time to explain why he couldn't sell me the horses instead of assuming I was a kid wasting his time and scolding me.

He seemed to be a nice person. ...But that didn't change the fact that he was pretty much helpless here.

"He says he's not selling you guys..." I said in horse language.

Wham! Wham!!!

"Ahhh!" Hang and Scary slammed their front hooves down upon the table, making the middle-aged manager fall backward from his chair.

"You can speak to horses...? D-Don't tell me you're Countess Raphael... No, I've heard she has scary-looking eyes, but I heard she's very old, and known as a monster..."

...Wait, I figured she'd be old, but "scary-looking eyes"?

Come to think of it, she did have an evil look on her face sometimes... That's it!

"Oh, are you familiar with my great grandmother?"

"Ah...?!"

Yes, it's working!

"Lady Kaoru, you should recite the three vows of the Silver breed to him! I've heard stories of a promise between Ed Silver the First, the manager at the time, and a noblewoman with a glare in her

CHAPTER 47: NEW DEPARTURE

eye and bad attitude. If we've heard of it, he must know about it too!"
Scary chimed in with some advice.

I had to give it a shot!

"The three vows of the Silver breed!"

"What...?" The manager looked flabbergasted. "I-It can't be...
That's just from folktales..."

"Breeehehe! Breeehehehe! (Hooray! Hooraaay!)"

We rode Hang and Scary out of the ranch to the sound of
boisterous cheers. The send-off was, of course, given by a crowd of
horses. The people from the administrative building saw us off too,
but they were either staring blankly or hanging their heads in silence.

...Um, sorry about that.

"I think we should be good now..." I said.

"What do you mean?" Reiko asked.

"Well, we're pretty far from the city now, so I was thinking of
bringing out the carriage..."

Both of us knew how to ride horses, but spending days or even
weeks on horseback would be tough. That was why I wanted to take
the journey in a carriage. We wouldn't need to worry about rain, and
we could sleep in the carriage when we were camping out. Though,
that said, I wouldn't make Hang and Scary walk in the rain, of
course. I'd have them take shelter under a tree or something.

"Oh, the Chariot thing..."

"No, a different one. That was..."

Yes, the Chariot was for Ed only. I had no intention of using it
with another horse.

"That was designed to be drawn by one horse, and it was for
me and Layette to ride when she was still little, so it's too small
for us. Plus, my companions rode horses, too, so it wasn't like they
needed to use it. I'm thinking of using one that's big enough for us

to lounge and sleep in this time... And it needs to be inconspicuous enough that we can ride it into the city..."

Yeah, the Chariot stood out too much because I had made it so cool-looking.

"Do you have any requests for the carriage?" I asked.

"No, not in particular. Make it however you'd like, Kaoru. Oh, but make sure it's comfortable to sit in."

Maybe Reiko had had a bad experience with one before, because she frowned and rubbed her butt as she said so. Carriages back on Earth weren't perfect, after all...

And so...

"Brehe! (Come out!) Brehehehehe! (Carriage of the Goddess!)" I chanted my incantation in horse language just for Hang and Scary. They should be able to recognize the carriage that serves as a vehicle of the Goddess, after all.

I was worried that they would be disappointed by its plain appearance, since I needed it to not stand out this time. I had a feeling they had big expectations about what it would look like.

Then...

Thud!

There appeared a brand-new carriage! There was a small barrel containing a potion in the interior, of course. ...I mean, the carriage wouldn't have been a "potion container" otherwise.

And although it looked like your average small carriage at first glance... Most of it was built with light and durable carbon nanotubes. Titanium had been used for some parts as well. Although titanium had many advantages, it was difficult and expensive to refine and process, so it was hard to use for large-scale construction. But since I could make objects appear in their completed form, that wasn't an issue for me.

Maybe if I really wanted to, I could have made a super special carriage, courtesy of Celes, with materials that didn't even exist on Earth. But I didn't really need to go that far. It was already made so it couldn't be pierced by arrows or spears, after all…

It had a coach box, which I could sit in and pretend to be the coachman when entering cities. Of course, it would actually be operated by giving verbal commands. I would be lonely sitting out there alone, so the coach box had room for two to sit side-by-side.

The cabin could be accessed directly from the coach box, and had two forward-facing seats and a rear-facing three-seat sofa with a table between them. The forward-facing seats came with headrests, and were designed to provide support for the entire body. We didn't want to strain our backs, after all.

You could even recline all the way back and go to sleep in comfort. This way, we could sleep while camping and while traveling. Though, one of us would obviously need to be awake for safety reasons.

I had to meet Hang and Scary's expectations, so I could even make a bunch of blades jut out with a pull of a lever. Without mechanisms like this, it would just be a normal carriage with high-quality materials. Well, the springs and the entire construction were rather unique, but I meant in terms of simple appearance. The blades probably weren't very practical; they really were just gimmicks to satisfy Hang and Scary.

Since this two-horse carriage was made to be much lighter than a normal carriage, it wouldn't be too much strain on the two of them. Though, they didn't seem to have the same reluctance Ed had about being a "carriage horse," so there probably wouldn't be any issues, anyway.

Wait… what if Ed started that whole rumor about only divine horses being able to pull the Goddess's carriage just to make them more eager to use it? Or maybe I was overthinking it? But Ed was considerate, and he had a strong sense of duty…

Dang, I'm getting sentimental again…

Ed would have wanted me to laugh rather than get all sappy remembering him. That's just the kind of horse he was. We were together for four and a half years… Four and a half years for a horse was like eighteen years for a human. Ed was six when I first met him, so he was about twenty-four in human years. Spending all our time together from twenty-four to forty-two would feel like an entire lifetime.

As for Hang and Scary's reaction…

"Ahhh, so this is the Goddess's carriage…"

"We're finally going to be divine horses, pulling the Goddess's carriage…"

They were getting all teary-eyed… But I didn't want to lie to them, so I decided to tell them the truth.

"That's not the same carriage that was drawn by Ed. That one was for Ed only… So I made this one specifically for the two of you. See how it's designed to be drawn by two horses?"

I was afraid they'd be disappointed to find out it wasn't the same one that had been used by their ancestor…

"What?! You made a brand-new carriage just for us? So this is our very own carriage… When we pass on someday, it will be preserved in the realm of gods for all eternity, and our deeds will live on forever…"

"Ahh! Ahh! Ahhh!"

They seemed to be happy about it, so I guess it was fine.

"Okay, then, let's go. Boarding!" I shouted like I was a sentai hero jumping into a giant robot and climbed into the carriage with Reiko.

Since we would be riding straight down the wide city streets, I decided we could just stay in the cabin. Any travelers we passed by may be surprised by the lack of a coachman at the front, but that wasn't too big of a deal. We could say the horses were well-trained, or we were using thin ropes to steer them from inside the cabin, or that we were in the middle of trying out a new carriage for military use. Anyone who questioned us would be assumed to be a spy, so I doubted they would bother us too much.

We each sat in one of the two front-facing seats… It looked like a gaming chair — which made sense, since that's what I was picturing when I made it…

"Move out!"

"…"

"…"

"……"

"We're not moving," Reiko said.

"Doesn't look like it…" I agreed. Why…?

"Lady Kaoru, how are we supposed to draw the carriage?" Hang asked from outside.

Ah… I forgot to hitch the horses to the carriage…

"…So, the fittings will come off if you just do this."

"…"

After hitching Hang and Scary to the carriage, I explained how they could remove the harness from the carriage on their own. It was designed so it could be disconnected this way, since it was easier for them to do with hooves compared to taking the harness off of their body. We might run into bandits or monsters, or the carriage could fall off a cliff during our travels. If they could disconnect their harnesses from the carriage in those cases, it would increase their odds of survival. That was why I added this feature, but…

The two horses seemed to be upset about something. Why?

"Y-You'd better not be thinking we might abandon the passengers and run away!" Hang yelled.

Huh?

"Even if it wasn't the Goddess riding in the carriage, we would never leave our passengers and try to run away, so you'd better not be thinking that!" Scary added.

Ah… Did I hurt their pride as professionals? Even Hang, who was relatively polite for a horse, was visibly displeased and spoke with rougher words. Come to think of it, Ed also got seriously upset whenever I said something that hurt his pride. Ed and his entire family put a lot of weight on pride and dignity.

Oh no, I screwed up…

"N-No, it's nothing like that! If we ever get attacked by bandits or monsters, you could disconnect your harnesses from the carriage and move next to the cabin so we can hop on and escape on your backs! I think it's a lot more convenient when you have the freedom to separate yourselves from the carriage when you deem it necessary. That's just how much I trust you two!"

"…Y-Yeah?"

"Hm, in that case, I suppose I could accept the idea…"

…Too easy.

Though, the real reason for having that function was so the horses could escape on their own in case the carriage flipped over, fell off a cliff, if we got surrounded and needed to use the carriage as a shield, or if Reiko and I needed to abandon the carriage and flee. I wasn't gonna let Ed's descendants die so easily.

And so, we were finally off. I was talking to Reiko in the cabin for some time, but we figured we should get to know the carriage first and headed out into the coach box. I was going to pretend to be driving as the coachman, so I had to get some practice in, too.

"Ah, Lady Kaoru. You know how to drive a carriage?"

"Lady Kaoru, there's no need to do that. We'll still walk, you know..." Hang and Scary said, but something felt off...

Oh, that's right... Ed...

"Hey, would you guys mind not calling me 'Lady Kaoru'?"

"What? Then should we call you Goddess?"

"No, just Kaoru, or Mi..."

"Mi?"

...Ed used to call me Missy. But it didn't feel right telling them to call me that...

"No, it's nothing. Call me what you want..."

"Very well, Lady Kaoru."

"You got it, Missy!"

"What...?" Hang called me Lady Kaoru just like before. As for Scary...

Hang had spoken pretty formally since we first met, while Scary was blunter with his words. Just like Ed...

"Wha! Such insolence!" Hang scolded Scary, appalled, but...

"No, that's fine. It gets a bit stuffy when you're too formal all the time."

"Gotcha!"

"..."

Hang looked rather conflicted, but it wasn't as if they both needed to address me the same way. They could each call me what they wanted.

And so, it was time to head east for now...

141

"Off we go!"

"...So, what about the name?" Reiko asked.

"Huh? Name?"

I was confused by her sudden question.

"I mean, you've always named everything since we were young, whether it was a snowboard or a rock you kicked on the way home. You're going to name this carriage too, aren't you? Just 'carriage' wouldn't be fit for our precious vehicle here."

"Urgh..."

It was true that I always gave names to things I grew attached to. I called Ed's carriage Chariot, and there was no need to rename it because there were no actual chariots around here. But our ride this time looked like a normal carriage in appearance, so I had been thinking that I needed to give it a proper name.

Hmm...

All right!

"I'll call it Merkava!"

"The name of a foreign tank?"

"No, they named it after the same reference. It actually means 'Chariot of God.'"

I didn't want a name that was too long, and I didn't want people to hear me calling it "Something of the Goddess." It'd be too embarrassing...

After continuing on for some time, the sun began to set.

"Is it okay if we camp out today? We're still some distance away from the next post town. The transaction at the ranch took up a whole lotta time..."

"Yeah. Using a tent is fine, too, but I want to see how comfortable it is sleeping in here. It's better to make use of new equipment like this while we can," Reiko responded, pretty much as expected.

And so, we went off of the street and into a thicket where we couldn't be spotted. We didn't want to be caught illegally camping out in the open, especially not somewhere we could be seen from the street. If you're gonna camp, you have to do it somewhere where you can't be seen.

We decided to sleep in the carriage without using the tent, as per Reiko's suggestion. Since we had some time, we decided to cook some dinner instead of pulling finished dishes out from the Item Box.

I brought out chairs and a table, a cooking table, a simple furnace, a water tank, cookware, and some ingredients, then got straight to making dinner.

I removed the harnesses from Hang and Scary and gave them some mixed feed with some carrots, corn, apples, sugar cubes, and potions.

"Ahh… This is the famous and legendary…"

"Yes, we're finally here, where the great Ed was once… To stand in the same position as our patriarch… So fortunate, so glorious!"

Ah, they're tearing up…

I thought horses rarely shed tears. I think Ed once told me that, didn't he…? Anyway, I was glad they seemed to be happy.

As I prepared to make some post-meal coffee after having dinner with Reiko, I opened the Item Box and…

Tweet tweet tweet tweet tweet! Tweet tweet tweet tweet tweet! Tweet tweet tweet tweet tweet!

"Huh?"

"What is it?" Reiko asked.

"The kids… Well, they're all old now, but… This is the ringtone for when the Eyes of the Goddess call me…"

I had a bad feeling about this. I was usually right about this sort of thing... Though, this wasn't just a "feeling." I was already sure of it. But I couldn't just ignore it...

And so, I reluctantly pulled the sound resonance crystal out of the Item Box.

The "potion container" crystal came in a pair, and I had given the other one to the Eyes of the Goddess when I first left the Kingdom of Balmore as a means of reaching out to me.

"This is Kaoru..." I cautiously spoke into the sound resonance crystal, then...

"Why would you do thiiiiiis?!"

My ears rang at the sudden burst of volume coming from the crystal.

"Why did you leave after just seeing Emile?! What in the world are you thinking?!"

Ah, that voice... Francette...

Emile must have invited Francette to dinner so he would get the scolding over with at once... He'd probably made the announcement after everyone had finished eating.

"Um... Is Emile..."

"Belle and Layette are beating him up behind me as we speak!"

I figured as much… They weren't young anymore, so they shouldn't get too reckless…

"Kaoru, I think I know what you're thinking, and you should tell them directly…" Reiko said.

It seemed Reiko and I still shared the ability to read each other's minds. From her point of view, Emile was just some old man she had met one time. Of course she'd be sympathetic, knowing he was getting mistreated. Reiko didn't know Francette, Belle, and Layette, after all…

"Please come back already!" Francette demanded. This didn't seem like the proper attitude to show to a goddess. She must have been preeetty mad…

But…

"…Sorry."

It was silent for some time.

"I'm sorry for being unreasonable…" she said.

"Huh? This isn't Francette. Are you an imposter or something?" I asked.

"Who are you calling an imposter?! I'm not a young woman anymore. I've changed since we last met!"

"Ah, sorry. It feels like just a few days ago to me…"

The Francette I knew had a pretty low threshold for flipping out. More silence followed…

Time felt really long in situations like these!

"Thank you for everything. You've given me such a h-happy li… life…" Francette was unable to speak coherently as she began to sob.

Oh no.

I'm not good at dealing with these things…

I just…

"How long are you going to hoard it? Let me talk to her!"

...Hm? Who was that? The voice sounded unfamiliar...

"Big Sis Kaoru!!!"

I-It's Layette!

I only knew her voice and speech patterns from when she was a little child, so of course I didn't recognize her...

I spoke with Francette, Layette, and each of the Eyes of the Goddess. They had matured by now and so much time had passed, so there weren't any tragic scenes or anything like that to speak of. Now that they were older, it seemed they were already past the grieving stage.

Even if we had met up again, it wasn't as if I could take care of them now that they were seniors. Their grandchildren could handle that.

I'll bet they made a bunch of descendants already! Tch!

All we could do now was reminisce about the past and be happy for each other's well-being. We talked, talked, and talked some more... Then I placed the now-silent sound resonance crystal back into the Item Box.

I wordlessly lay on the grass with my back turned toward Reiko, then I heard her settling down on the ground a short distance away. She probably had her back to me, too. We had agreed to sleep in the carriage tonight, but it seemed she was okay with sleeping out on the grass with me like this. I didn't want to sleep inside the carriage, because she would be able to hear me sobbing.

...*That's my Reiko.*

Reiko Kuon, one of my only two best friends. And now, she was just Reiko... My friend.

"I'm baaack!" I woke up energetically the next morning.

Reiko gave me a look, but I didn't care. She already knew how brash I could be, and how quickly I could recover from feeling down.

Animals were early risers, so Hang and Scary were already up. So, I decided to get them some breakfast and water. I felt like it wouldn't be healthy to depart right after waking up, so better to eat first. I could have brought some pre-cooked food out of my Item Box, but I went ahead and started boiling some water. It would have been too easy to pull some already-boiling water out, after all. Though, I was using a portable gas cartridge stove instead of building a furnace out of rocks or collecting firewood, so it was easy enough already.

I had made various types of potion container stoves that used alcohol, oil, or gasoline as fuel, along with wood stoves, but I felt like using the gas cartridge stove. It was the quickest and easiest to use, after all.

...One might wonder why I had prepared so many different types of camping stoves. I just like camping goods, okay?! I had never gone camping before, but I still bought several books about that stuff! So what? ...The water and pot came from the Item Box, too. I didn't feel like making "a pot with water in it" every time, and I would end up with more and more pots if I did that...

Even though there was no limit to the Item Box's capacity, I didn't want it to be stuffed with a bunch of cheap pots.

I quickly made breakfast, and as we ate together...

"Sorry for spending so much time talking to my old friends yesterday..."

I had to apologize to Reiko. I knew she didn't mind such things, but that was exactly why I had to. I didn't want to take advantage of the fact that it wouldn't be an issue if I didn't apologize.

"No, it's okay. You were saying goodbye to the people you care about. I can be with you from here on, so of course you were supposed to prioritize your time with them yesterday."

That was exactly what I had expected Reiko to say. After all, we only had a little bit of time to talk when I died and asked the Earth God to let me say goodbye in her dream. She knew the importance of time spent saying farewell to loved ones. But there was a huge difference between putting your thoughts into words and not saying anything at all. We were such close friends that we understood each other without saying these things, but that was all the more reason to say them.

Oh, that's right...

"Hey, Reiko, can you use the magic powers you got to make food, camping tools, guns, and tanks?" I had to ask.

Her magic probably wasn't the actual "magic" that most people thought of. I had a suspicion that, just like with my powers, there was some being below Celes that was subcontracted or sub-subcontracted by Celes to handle it, or maybe a highly advanced robot or AI that was controlling some scientific element to make things happen...

The only time I had seen Reiko's magic was that time she created water to put out my fire.

Burn, baby, burn... Wait, shaddap!

"Of course not! What kind of magic is that? It can't do anything so ludicrous that it exceeds the realm of 'normal magic.' I may be able to use any magic, but it's limited to fire magic, water magic, wind magic, and earth magic. I can't travel through space or create things, or bring the dead back to life or anything crazy like that…"

"Ah, thought so… Guess even Celes isn't *that*…you know. Though, magic that could bend space would be asking to create distortions, so I guess I shouldn't be surprised…"

I did refrain from explicitly speaking ill of Celes. I didn't want a wooden pail to be dropped on my head again. It REALLY hurts, you know…

In any case, it was just as I expected. If there were no limits to what she could do with magic, she could create literally anything, bring things from Earth here, and travel to and from Earth by saying it was all "creation magic," "alternate world network super magic," or "dimensional transportation magic."

That would have been too much, and I couldn't imagine Celes agreeing. Something like that would basically make her super OP.

Though, being able to create water and fire meant she'd be fine out in the wild, and having powerful offensive magic at her disposal would let her fend off bandit attacks without worries. She had the same ability to understand languages and an Item Box like me, too…

What a cheater!!!

Though, really, I guess I shouldn't be talking. I could probably do those things. I could create a tank-type container, or a firearm-type container… I wouldn't know how to use them, though.

It wasn't as if I knew how to drive a tank, or operate its weapons. Even if I could make an attack helicopter, I didn't know how to make it fly, either…

Maybe Celes had learned her lesson with me and decided not to give out cheat powers that were too powerful… Though, the

Item Box in itself was pretty ridiculous. It could really hurt the logistics industry, too...

Though, it'd be fine as long as we didn't try to make a business out of it. Magic was only observed on a small scale in this world, so the magic Reiko could use was already a cheat power. And...

"Don't you think you might be persecuted as a witch or a demon if you use your magic in this world?" I asked Reiko.

"Ah..."

She could use fire and water magic in a world where magic was pretty much nonexistent. Plus, they would mainly be used to cause destruction. Not to mention, the Goddess was real in this world. Therefore, even though they didn't exist and no one had seen one before, people believed demons existed as a counterpart to the Goddess.

"..."

This was bad.

"..."

Real bad.

The reason I was able to get by relatively undisturbed, despite getting involved in so much trouble and revealing my superhuman powers, was because I was thought to be Celes's errand girl. But what if it was the opposite, and they thought Reiko was an errand girl of Celes's enemy, a demon? It would be time for a fun little witch-hunting party. The main dish? Barbecue...

"Never use magic where you can be seen until you secure a position where you're absolutely safe to use it, or when you're sure you can kill all witnesses! ...Except in emergencies, that is."

Nod, nod!

I was glad to see Reiko understood the potential danger she was in. But now we were pretty much just two underage girls traveling via horse and carriage with no guards. We weren't just a perfect target for thieves, but merchants, travelers, and even rural villagers might have some unscrupulous ideas if they came across us...

Even just the carriage and two horses would fetch a pretty penny. Considering we were just two young girls, we looked like airheaded heiresses from rich families, oblivious to the dangers of the world. We could have money and jewelry on us, and could be exchanged for ransom or sold to traffickers...

Uh-oh, we were far too tempting as targets. Though, that would always be the case. No one would be able to tell that Reiko could easily fend off attackers until we actually got attacked. As such, we would always appear to be the perfect prey.

I should have known! Ahaha! ...Like hell!

This was bad. We had to do something. We had to make it harder for attackers to target us, and find a way for us to dispatch attackers that wouldn't put us in a bad position.

"All right, let's upgrade our armaments!"

That was our only choice. We needed a carriage that was threatening enough to discourage attackers, despite the fact that it was just two girls inside, but it couldn't draw too much attention in the city. It was a tall order...

What should I do...?

As we talked in horse language so as not to exclude Hang and Scary from the conversation, Hang spoke to us from behind.

"Excuse me...but maybe instead of going out of our way to use one carriage that fits both requirements, can't we switch between one for using in the city and one for the road?"

"Oh..."

I didn't expect to be outwitted by a horse...

And so, we decided to use three separate carriages.

Panzer was an armored combat vehicle for the roads. The interior was basically the same as Merkava, but the exterior looked like a military armored carriage with spears and swords loaded onto it. It was a bluff to make it seem like soldiers would jump out and fight if something was to happen. I didn't feel like moving the long spears and swords in and out every time, so we just strapped them down to the exterior...

Plus, there were gun ports facing every direction. Of course, we would shoot Reiko's fire or water magic out of those instead of using actual guns. The ports weren't necessary for magic attacks, but they were there so we could use excuses like having sprayed burning oil or firing water out of a pump. We would decline to explain further and claim it was a trade secret.

We would use Merkava when traveling through areas that weren't too dangerous, or when riding with other carriages. That way, we wouldn't stand out too much compared to the others...

And for riding in the city, we had Penelope, a slightly fancy small carriage that might have been used by a middle-class merchant family. Despite its name, it had four wheels instead of six.

Okay, all set! To the east we go!

Chapter 48:
Heading East

"...So, what's our destination?"

"The enemy super-dreadnought!"

" "
...

" "
...

Crickets...

"We're going east. Most of the people who have met me in person probably aren't alive anymore, but I have a lot of old connections in the countries around here... If I'm gonna leave the past in the past and start a new life with you, I want to build a foundation someplace far away, instead of putting it in countries on this peninsula. That way, it'll be completely uncharted territory for both of us, and we can start over from scratch. I'm sure most people haven't heard about me there, or they've only heard false rumors that have been warped over time, so I should be able to lay low.

"Let's find some decent place to put down roots for a while. If we don't like where we end up, we can always move again. We have plenty of time, after all."

Exchange of information took a very long time in this world, and its details tended to change drastically in the process. Rumors would completely lose their original content very quickly, so no one actually believed anything that came from a faraway land. They might discuss those rumors for fun, but they still assumed them to be untrue. So, considering the magnitude of the events of the past, those rumors were surely known throughout the continent already. But it was highly unlikely anyone remembered any accurate information that was over seventy years old.

"That's true. Kyoko didn't seem like she had much longer, either…"

Huh?

"How is Kyoko…?"

"Oh, the last time I saw her was about two years ago. Neither of us were in any shape to be going out after that… I was hooked up to IVs and oxygen tubes. Kyoko didn't need any, but she still couldn't be out and about by herself."

"Just how old were you two?!"

They probably had a bunch of kids, too. Damn them…

We had a meeting inside the carriage — I mean, the Panzer — about what our plans were going to be, moving forward.

We made our way out of the peninsula and through the center of the continent, toward the coast on the other side. I had to be by the sea as a Japanese person, after all… I mean, you were relatively close to the sea no matter where you lived in Japan, and you could get fresh seafood any time you wanted, but only dried seafood was available inland here. This was pretty rough for a Japanese person. So, I preferred to live by the seaside.

We could go fishing or dig for clams, or even go out for a swim. Besides, there was no reason to live far away from the sea when we could go anywhere we wanted.

And so, we made our way through the Kingdom of Brancott and toward Drisard. I had caused some trouble immediately after entering Drisard last time, so we had to quickly change directions southward to the Kingdom of Jusral, which was close to the border.

We didn't need to worry about that this time, so we planned on continuing to the east.

I had only stayed in the region briefly, outside of the kidnapping incident, so I doubted anyone would recognize me in Drisard, or even in the entire Kingdom of Brancott. Case in point: after being rescued out of the Item Box, I went by completely undetected on my way to the Kingdom of Balmore. Even though my name and appearance had been recorded for religious purposes, everyone's memories and information had greatly degraded over time. Not to mention, there weren't any photos or even portraits drawn with me as a model. Pictures drawn from memory, usually after getting a glimpse of me from a distance, couldn't have been very accurate.

So, while we didn't experience any issues as we kept moving east, we still decided to sit side-by-side in the coach box, without doing anything funny, until we got through Balmore and Brancott just in case.

Once we pass through both, I could put up a notice saying, "Testing automated driving features," or "This carriage is currently propelled by nuclear power."

Then I realized that travelers who saw a carriage moving forward without a driver would either assume the horses were walking on their own, after the driver had a seizure and fell out, or they had started walking forward while the driver was gone. Either way, they might try to take it for themselves.

It was no good...

But I didn't feel like sitting in the coach box the entire time, and two kids sitting in the front would have been a bad-guy magnet, too...

The two humans and two horses racked our brains to come up with a plan...

"Yeah, this should work!"

"They're definitely a normal driver and a guard."

Yes, we decided to put stuffed dummies in the coach box! One looked like a driver, and the other looked like a guard. This would also make it seem as if there were more guards inside.

The perfect plan!

We made it through the Kingdom of Brancott without issues, and our driverless carriage problem was resolved by putting our dummies, Shunsuke and Oscar, in the coach box.

We wouldn't be by the sea for a while, but I had seafood stocked up in my Item Box, so that wasn't an issue. ...It was from seventy-three years ago, but it wasn't as if it would age or rot. But it still felt weird knowing that, so I decided to donate it to an orphanage somewhere on the way and restock. They would appreciate the seafood less the closer they were to the shore, so I had to donate it on the way, with the intention of running out around the time I got to the coastal area.

And so, after we hurriedly moved through Balmore and Brancott without stopping or resting, we went at a leisurely pace, camping out once for every three nights or so that we stayed at an inn. It wasn't as if I particularly loved to camp, and I had absolutely nothing to do when we did. Camping wasn't completely safe, for one thing, and I wanted to have access to a proper meal and bath. Camping out because the next town was too far was fine, but there was no reason to do so all the time.

Plus, going from point A to point B with no stops along the way felt too dry. It was pointless if we couldn't stop somewhere for a few days along the way to enjoy the trip. Fortunately, we both had plenty of time, and we couldn't have Hang and Scary pulling the carriage every day. We had to let them rest up here and there.

So...

"All right, let's spend a few days in the next city!"

"Agreed!"

Reiko was on board, so it was decided. There was no reason to rush, so I elected to enjoy the rest of the journey at my leisure. I decided to leave the carriage, Hang, and Scary at the horse stables while we stayed in cities. The barns at most inns were too small, and while they did care for horses there, their services were just adequate. Horses preferred to be under the care of specialists. That's what Ed told me, anyway. I mean, all they could do at inns was provide feed and water.

On the other hand, horse care professionals would wash, dry, brush, and check the horse's legs and overall health for anything out of the ordinary. They even changed out the straw regularly... When leaving horses at stables over a long time, the stablemaster will often confirm which day the carriage will be needed and give them some exercise at pasture during open days. Though, that would obviously cost extra...

I was only planning on leaving the horses for a few days this time, and I wouldn't need the carriage during the stay, so I left the horses' care until the departure day in the hands of the staff at the stables. I could have stuffed the horses and carriage in my Item Box, but I would've felt bad for Hang and Scary, so I scrapped that idea. The two wouldn't have been able to rest if I did that, anyway.

Sure, I could have put just the carriage in the Item Box, but it would have been unnatural if Reiko and I rode around bareback, and it wasn't too expensive to store carriages, anyway. I was pretty rich, after all.

I found a secluded area and switched carriages from Panzer to the Penelope, put the two dummies back in the Item Box, then Reiko and I sat out in the coach box. We now looked like two daughters of a wealthy merchant family out on a leisurely jaunt.

I had already gone into cities like this many times. The only thing different this time was that I would have to stop by the stables to leave the horses and carriage instead of going straight to an inn. Tonight, we were staying at a somewhat fancy inn with a proper bath. It was just us two girls, so we had to prioritize our safety.

I was ready to enjoy my first restful stay since escaping from the Item Box!

"I will see you in three days, then. I'll contact you if I need to extend the duration…"

"Very well. Please enjoy your stay."

I finished handing over Hang and Scary, along with the carriage, and paid an additional fee to upgrade their care and meals. It wasn't like horses could take a bath like us, so meals were the only thing they had to look forward to. I wasn't gonna skimp out on something like that.

That reminded me, I had to stop by a store to stock up on their food… Even I didn't have several months' worth of horse feed stocked up at all times. My reserve was starting to run low. So, I decided to buy a little more than usual this time.

I would need funds for the inn and other expenses, so our next stop was…

"What…?"

I went to exchange some of my old coins for the current… the Kaorun gold coins, but the attendant reacted with surprise.

"So many…"

Banks and money-changers shouldn't act so surprised at seeing a little bit of gold! It was a pretty unprofessional reaction…

After exchanging a decent amount of coins, we headed out to secure our inn. I actually wanted to exchange a lot more, but we would draw attention if we used too much money at once, and it was all the more suspicious coming from a young girl like me. We left quickly, before anyone started making arrangements to trail us.

There was no need for me to exchange all my money at once. I just needed enough to hold me over for now, and I could take care of the rest later. The priority, for now, was to secure our inn for the night.

We were in a decent-sized city, so there were several inns to choose from, but I wanted to choose one that was relatively high-end. Regardless of how old we were on the inside, we did look like two frail little girls, after all. We definitely didn't need any weirdos messing with us.

Money is earned to be saved, but also to be used when necessary. When else would we use it if not to enjoy our journey comfortably? That's why I wasn't stingy when it came to paying for lodging and food, even though I was strict with budgeting for usual living expenses.

"Do you have any rooms for two available?"

"Why, yes, we do. How long would you like to stay?"

"Three nights, for now. I'll let you know beforehand if we need to extend our stay."

The receptionist treated us with respect despite us looking like two kids, as expected of a somewhat high-end inn. We were wearing pretty nice clothes, so that may have helped. Unfortunately, it looked like they didn't have a bath after all. Only very high-end inns had baths readily available.

I let Reiko handle the talking at the inn. I knew more about how inns worked in this world, but you know...

In this world, I looked like I was about twelve or thirteen, or even eleven. But Reiko could pass for a fourteen- or fifteen-year-old. That's why the staff at the inn looked at Reiko whenever we talked, so she just naturally ended up taking care of the proceedings. This was the case whenever we went shopping, too. We were about the same in height, so what was up with that...? Was it because I had a young-looking face?

...No, I know. Don't say it!

Did the people of this world judge women's ages by the size of their breasts? Damn it!

We received our key and made our way to our room upstairs.

"Should I cast some cleaning magic?" Reiko asked.

"Please!"

There was no bath here, but we were fine because we had Reiko's magic. Previously, I just used my powers to make a hot potion with cleaning and anti-bacterial properties inside a metal basin, so I would've been fine, anyway. Still, as a Japanese person, there were times when I just wanted to have a nice soak in a bathtub. I remember going on an impulsive journey to find hot springs and ending up getting involved in some trouble...

Anyway.

"Tomorrow and the day after, we go sightseeing. Then we leave on the third day. Sound good?" I asked.

"Okay!"

And three days later, we headed east again.

...What? Nothing happened till then! It wasn't like there were any interesting buildings, amusement centers, or well-maintained tourist facilities in this world...

Yeah, I had already expected that. Sure, there were beautiful sights and lots of nature, but most of this world was filled with nature, and we weren't gonna come across anything particularly interesting

161

just because we had traveled a short distance away from civilization. If we went to the mountains or an unexplored region, maybe we'd have run into some waterfalls, lakes, or some other majestic sights, but we didn't intend to go too far out of our way like that. We could do that sort of thing after things settled down and we had a lot of excess time on our hands.

And so, we ended up staying for two or three days to let Hang and Scary rest up, then continued eastward, without having high expectations for any sights we might come across on the way...

"It's the sea..."

"It's the sea all right."

"S-So, this is..."

"The legendary sea..."

Well, maybe we were being a bit dramatic.

In any case, we arrived at our destination: the coast on the eastern side of the continent. I ended up skipping over the ride because nothing really happened along the way, but many days had passed since we left the Kingdom of Balmore. People had heard about the incident from seventy years ago way out here, but they were just tall tales and horribly inaccurate stories from a distant land, so it was unlikely that anyone even knew about the names or appearances of anyone involved. Not to mention, it was possible that most ordinary people hadn't even heard of something from so many decades ago.

In other words, I didn't have to worry about being recognized here.

"So, let's go on as planned and..."

"Yeah, let's set up our home base at a decent-sized port town!"

Yes, it was time to set up our home base. I wanted to live as a normal resident of this world, but I didn't want to go out of my way to experience hardship or inconvenience. However, if my living situation was too far out of the ordinary, it could end up being a hindrance when other people took notice of me.

That's why I decided to secure a house instead of living at an inn. I also wanted to buy it instead of renting, so I could do whatever I wanted with it. Renting a place left me open to people trying some funny business, like what happened with Layette's Atelier. Sure, I could crush such annoyances easily, but I didn't want to deal with that, or possibly have to leave this country as a consequence...

I guess you could say my priority was avoiding trouble rather than worrying about losing money. I wasn't too concerned with money in the first place, anyway. I had plenty of gold coins, but I really just wanted to live a normal life, and I didn't intend to just lie around doing nothing all day. Such a life would not only be boring, but it would negatively impact my efforts in finding a husband. Yup.

I mean, I could kill time lying around if I had the internet, but the internet, TV, books, and manga didn't exist in this world... Of course I'd get bored pretty quickly.

I had exchanged a lot of coins on the way here. Whenever we went to a city with a money changer, I exchanged my coins right before departing to the next destination, instead of doing it as soon as I arrived. It turns out I was pretty wealthy from all the potion sales and new products I made in collaboration with the Abili Trade Company, and most of those funds had been stored in my Item Box as gold coins. The rest of my holdings consisted entirely of the house I had given to the kids of the Eyes of the Goddess.

After exchanging a bunch of money in each city, we had moved right on to the next one. Even if someone came after us, we were riding on the small and lightweight Penelope, drawn by two top-class Silver horses powered up with potions, so there was no way anyone on foot or in an ordinary carriage could catch up to us. If someone did manage to catch up to us on horseback, we would swap from the delicate Penelope into the bulky Panzer, and our dummies would be sitting in the coach box instead of two little girls.

Because of that, there were several times when some rough-looking gentlemen rode past us on horseback, but we didn't get dragged into trouble even once. It goes without saying that we left the dummies out in the coach box and didn't stop by any cities until we made sure the grumpy-looking men passed by us again on their way back to the city they had come from. We made sure to stay cautious about things like this.

I exchanged my old money for Kaorun gold coins up until we reached the Drisard region, but from there on, they were exchanged for the gold coins used in each respective country. That understandable, and I didn't really mind. I was going to exchange them again once we chose a place to settle, anyway. If I turned in a pile of ancient coins at the place I wanted to stay, people might assume I found a fortune in some cave or something and end up causing a commotion. That was why I converted them all into modern currency.

It was extra work on my part, and I'd lose a percentage of my holdings with the exchange fee, but that couldn't be helped. That was a small price to pay for safety and avoiding trouble.

"How about we say this is our top candidate for now and see how things go for a while? We could stay at an inn in the meantime," I suggested.

"Yeah. We arrived at this port town going down the main road, so I'm pretty sure this is a major city in this region. There's no reason to pass through here and go out of our way to a different city now."

It seemed Reiko was on the same page.

And so, the trial period to see if this would be our new home and city of new beginnings had begun!

Chapter 49:
Port Town Tarvolas

The place we booked was just your run-of-the-mill inn. The reception area and the dining-room-slash-tavern were on the first floor, with the living area for the owner's family in the back. The second and third floors housed the guest rooms. I felt like the owner's family space was pretty small, but come to think of it, they could use the same kitchen, bathroom, and other facilities as the guests, so maybe they didn't need too much family space.

The reason I hadn't prioritized safety and gone for a higher-end inn this time was because I wanted to see what the standard of living was like for the average person in this city. I didn't want to live in a place that was dangerous or full of problems. If the city was ruled by a crime syndicate or full of thugs roaming the street, I'd like to know... That's why I went with a completely ordinary place rather than lodgings for rich people.

...Still, I wasn't reckless enough to stay at a low-class inn when we appeared to be just two young girls. Sure, Reiko and I could handle ourselves with my potions and her magic, but we'd be forced to leave the country if anyone saw us. I didn't want any trouble.

So, here we were, in an ordinary room at an ordinary inn. Our room was on the third floor. The bathroom was on the first floor, so it was a pain to descend and climb the stairs every time, but considering that the tavern was also on the first floor, they probably assigned us to the third floor out of courtesy. It wasn't as if we needed to use the bathroom all the time, anyway.

"Let's walk around for a week or so and check out the city while looking for our future home," I suggested.

"Yeah. We should figure out what to do for work, too," Reiko said.

Yes, we hadn't decided what sort of work we would do yet. I had put that off because I wanted to find work that we could do that was a good fit for the city and would prove useful for the residents there. Of course, physical labor and time-consuming jobs were out of the question. It wasn't as if I was desperate for money, so I didn't want all my time being bound up in a job.

I mean, we had plenty of time with a long life ahead of us, but that didn't mean I was okay with living a lifestyle I wasn't happy with. I didn't want to run a shop because of how much time I would need to spend there. No thanks to anything that required a lot of prep time, and no way was I gonna deal with anything that could draw attention from the rich and powerful. I didn't want anything that would keep me really busy or require me to maintain annoying relationships with trading partners, either.

I could just use my cheat powers and make easy money...no, I want to help others.

Anyway, whether we would stay in this city and the type of lifestyle we would have depended on the intel we were about to gather. She who controls information controls the world, as they say.

Six days later...

"I think we checked out just about everywhere..."

"Yeah. We only looked into what a foreign commoner could, but I think we got enough information to determine the city's atmosphere, level of safety, the residents' sense of morals, and the general policies here," Reiko agreed.

And...

"I like it!"

The lord of this area was a count who not only understood his privileges as an aristocrat, but was also aware of his duties. That was why it was safe and peaceful here. ...By this world's standards, that is.

The king supposedly took his job seriously too... Maybe that was why a respectable aristocrat was the lord of this territory? In any case, I had no complaints about the kingdom, lord, or city. We could probably find other cities in other countries that were on par with this place, but it would be hard to find anything that was significantly better. That meant there was no reason to take a risk and continue our journey.

"Okay, let's live here!"

"Agreed. We can always move again if things don't work out."

And so, we decided to settle in the port town of Tarvolas.

I bought a house in the suburbs. ...Okay, maybe that was a bit abrupt.

The center of the city was packed with buildings used as storefronts, work areas, and residences. There were some vacant buildings too, but they were either rentals; didn't fit my criteria in terms of size, available facilities, location, or price; or the realtor chased me away as soon as they saw us...

I mean, judging by our appearance, I couldn't blame them if they thought we were just kids wasting their time. We had no issues buying this place when I showed them a bag full of gold coins, though.

What? I should have done that in the first place? I couldn't just flash a bag stuffed with money when I didn't even know if I was going to buy the place yet, or whether I was dealing with a legitimate seller... I'd have been a prime target for con artists and criminals.

Come to think of it, Roland was around to help with the proceedings for leasing Layette's Atelier and Convenience Store Belle. Roland was pretty useful once in a while after all... Now it was just two (seemingly) young girls.

Anyway, we planned on going through several realtors to have them introduce some properties to us, but that didn't go too well. Next, we looked for a vacant property we liked ourselves, researched the market price in the area, then searched for the realtor who was handling that property. We asked all around the city, but...

First off, any place that was too small was an automatic no. It wasn't like we were tight on money, so even though we were close friends, I couldn't deal with a lack of privacy. I also had to have a working kitchen, bathtub, toilet, drainage, and other plumbing-related amenities. No rooms that could be peered into from the outside. Nothing that would invite loud noises, foul odors, or deterioration of public order in the area. I mean, living next to a blacksmith or tavern would mean dealing with noise early in the morning or late at night. Lack of sleep and stress was bad for the skin, after all.

And the most important requirement was the ability to maintain secrecy. I couldn't live in an area where it was common for the lady next door to come into my house without knocking to share some leftovers. It wasn't that I disliked having such warmhearted connections with people, but I planned on having a bunch of convenient things in my place...

This was the property we ended up finding: a former orphanage. Currently empty, it was a not-too-run-down one-story house built atop a cliff about twenty meters or so above sea level. Despite only having one floor, it was pretty big. There was a lot of open land here, but it took specific skills to build two-story houses, and there was no reason to get one considering how dangerous it was to fix the roof of such buildings ourselves. I figured we'd be on our own if we had to fix a leak in the roof...

Plus, since it used to be an orphanage, it made sense to make it a one-story house to lower the chance of accidents with so many little rascals running around all the time. There were many rooms in this building of different sizes, so I figured we would have the option to put them to different uses. A normal-sized private house wasn't gonna be big enough to use as our home base.

Besides, the true value of a base wasn't about what was above ground, but below. That the property was in the suburbs with a big lot was convenient for us. Building a secret base under a 900 square meter house in the middle of the city wasn't very realistic, after all...

Not to mention, the price was very affordable. I mean, what normal buyer would want to live in a former orphanage with such peculiar architecture?

So, I paid it off in cash and that was that. We just had to have some professional fix it up, then build a basement to upgrade with magic. How am I going to make a basement, you ask?

With the Item Box and Reiko's magic, anything is possible!

I had a contractor come in, not only to do repairs, but for some additional work, as well. The biggest thing I had them do was make one-meter-square storage chambers under the floorboards of my room, Reiko's room, and several other areas in the house.

He did wonder why we wanted to make such small chambers when we had so many available rooms, but I explained that we wanted to store condiments and non-perishables in a cool place, and he seemed to buy that.

Of course, their real purpose wasn't to store anything, but to use them as secret entrances. We would be making basements under the building, so we would be using these as hidden passageways to get in and out of there. An entrance that looked like normal flooring when closed couldn't really be made as a potion container, and Reiko's earth magic wasn't much help there, either. That's why we had some professional help.

We also had wooden windows, so I wanted to change them for glass, but I endured that for now. I didn't want to appear too wealthy right off the bat, or we might draw some unwanted attention. A glass window was just inviting thieves to come right in.

…Then again, buying such a building (along with the land) with cash was already pretty telling, but we didn't have any choice but to pay with cash as two young outsiders, so there wasn't much we could do about that. As such, we would at least act as if we had used all of our money to buy this place, leaving us broke. That was why we had to start working right away.

Anyway, I wanted to get all the necessary furniture first. We still had everything the previous owners of the house had been using. It was one thing to buy a shop with all of its equipment, interiors, fixtures, and furnishings included, but we really wished they hadn't left all of their personal goods. There was plenty of space, so we decided to get rid of the old furniture and equipment later and focus on buying stuff we needed for now.

"…Ready?"

"Yup!"

It was the dead of night. Anyone looking from the outside wouldn't have been able to tell what we were doing, but we still made sure no one was around before getting to work.

"Storing!"

I stored away the dirt and rocks underground as we worked on making the basement. We had to make sure we didn't expand too far, in order to keep the building above from collapsing. We left pillars and walls for support rather than completely hollowing it out, and used Reiko's earth magic for reinforcement. Apparently, her magic could harden dirt so that it was like stone.

Then we expanded sideways by adding a few rooms.

…This was step one.

Then we dug diagonally downwards by using the Item Box to store more dirt, moving at an angle away from directly below the building, and ran into bedrock. We proceeded to extend the passageway into the rock and began building our underground area proper there. Instead of making one giant room, we divided the space into several rooms to maintain its structural integrity. Of course, Reiko reinforced each of them, just in case.

Yes, that first basement served as a sort of decoy. Anyone searching the house would be satisfied if they found it, thinking they'd discovered the secret room and its few gold coins stored there, never suspecting that there was another hidden basement. It was just human nature.

That said, we would still be storing stuff there, and it could still be used as a hidden room, so it wasn't as if it was going to waste. It goes without saying that we had been digging in the direction away from the sea. If we had gone the opposite way, we would have dug through the cliff and out the other side.

This time, we changed direction toward the sea. We made our way diagonally downward, closer to the sea surface. We then continued our digging below the sea, so we could connect to the sea floor from underground. This way, we could fish and swim underground without going outside... No, it was to be used as a secret escape path. If we put a submersible boat down there, we could safely flee even if we were surrounded by enemies.

I highly doubted our enemies would predict this and have boats waiting for us out on the sea, and even if they did, we could still get away with a submersible. If Kyoko was around, she'd have chimed in saying, "Just who are you fighting with here?!" but unfortunately, Reiko and I were the same type of person when it came to this sort of thing. We were big proponents of going out of our way to prepare things "just in case." It was just in our nature...

We took the ebb and flow of the tide into account and built a waterway connected to the sea, then withdrew for now.

On the way back, I used the Item Box to make detailed adjustments on the corridor I dug out, staircasing the pathway as Reiko reinforced it with earth magic, making it easier to walk on. If we hadn't done that, we were just asking to trip and slide all the way down eventually. I mean, we could also trip on the stairs, but still...

We ended the day after building the rooms and corridors. With the major construction work out of the way, all that was left was to make small adjustments as we installed the furniture.

We finished most of the work within a few days. The basement directly under the floor of the house was used for storing unneeded goods, like the stuff the previous residents had left behind, non-perishable food, consumables, and rooms for when unwelcome visitors happened to come by. I could put all of our resources into the Item Box, but it was best to be prepared for unexpected situations. It wasn't as if we went out to the city to shop every day, so it would have been strange for us not to have certain things stocked up.

We had installed a bunch of things in the main base in the bedrock and along the escape path into the sea. Yes, all sorts of "potion containers"…

Reiko was exasperated as she complained, "My magic isn't much of a cheat power compared to this!" but never mind that. It was difficult to make the above-ground areas completely impenetrable, so we made arrangements to make them not stand out if someone happened to catch a glimpse of them. Anything that could draw unwanted attention was moved underground.

Although I wanted to enjoy modern conveniences, I couldn't just put air conditioning or a TV right out in the open. I merely wanted to enhance the lifestyle of this world, not recreate life back on Earth. We were no longer the Japanese women known as Kaoru Nagase and Reiko Kuon, but residents of this world, Kaoru and Reiko.

So, we had purchased our beds in the city, and bought all of our other daily necessities normally. We had to contribute to the economy, so we couldn't just hoard gold coins in the Item Box forever. I wanted to do anything that could be done through normal means normally.

Still, there were some things I couldn't compromise on. That's why we had been using potion containers for cookware and chairs. No way was I gonna light logs in a stove every time I wanted to make something! Who would want to cook with such an unstable heat source?! Sure, all of the chefs and housewives in this world cooked with this method, but it was too much for us.

…And chairs are very important! This is a key point, so I'll say it again. Chairs are very important! I mean, I could just drink a potion if I hurt my back, but still…

And then there was laundry. We obviously weren't using a fully automatic washing machine or dryer. They would have been way too out of place… But I wasn't about to use a laundry tub and washboard to scrub my clothes, either. It was too much work, and it damaged the fabric.

Yes, there was a convenient solution. I could just store my clothes in the Item Box and order it to remove any dirt particles. But I didn't want to do that. It didn't feel right.

And so, I decided to put my clothes in a laundry tub and step on them. I was using a potion that would instantly remove dirt, so I just had to step on them a few times and it'd be done with.

…One could say that my solution wasn't much better than using the Item Box to clean my clothes.

I don't care, as long as it looks fine if people see me!

We had been using the water from a channel that was dug from a nearby stream. Of course, it wasn't as if we could get underground water by digging a bit into the cliff we were on. Below an old manor atop a rocky mountain is a raging underground river… No, this wasn't some swashbuckling novel from the Taisho era… Where would the water be coming from on top of a rocky mountain, anyway?

As for that channel we had been using, it seemed the previous residents here had dug it out. It was completely uncovered, so it was full of leaves and debris. Using it for laundry and bathing was one thing, but I wasn't quite brave enough to drink it, so I added a device to filter and sterilize the water.

Of course, wastewater was sent into the sea through a cleaning unit (potion container) underground.

Now we're all set!

The story of the little girls who bought the land and building from the former orphanage had probably spread to some degree already. When paying the realtor and the contractor, I had emphasized that we had used up all of our savings buying and fixing up this place, so we needed to work to support ourselves. The gossip lovers of the city, starved for entertainment, were sure to be curious about the mysterious girls who had just arrived, so there was no way they wouldn't ask the realtor and contractor about us. They in turn would prioritize their relationships with their neighbors over the privacy of their clients.

I decided to see how things went for another week or two. From there, I could take my time figuring out an easy job that wasn't too time-consuming, wouldn't draw attention from weirdos, and would earn me enough that I could make somewhat expensive purchases without looking suspicious.

There was a time when I believed that, anyway...

Chapter 50:
Yeah... I Thought So

Ring ring, ring ring, ring ring!

"Intruders!"

One night, the alarm system in our property detected invaders on the premises. It may have just been a normal visitor or a wild animal, but it was generally best to expect the worst in these situations.

...And, even then, reality tended to take you by surprise.

I was relaxing in the living room with Reiko at the time, so our response was quick. I checked the position of the sensor potion container that detected the intruder using the surveillance panel potion container. I aimed the infrared camera potion container that I had installed on the roof and zoomed in. Then I used the LCD monitor potion container to...

Okay, enough! I'm skipping the "potion container" stuff from now on!

Anything that shouldn't exist in this world was made as a potion container! I don't compromise when it comes to our safety! Safety first. That went without saying!

And on the monitor, we saw...

"Kids?"

I saw a boy who was about five or six years old and a girl around ten years old on the monitor. The two looked around cautiously as they slowly approached the building. They looked a little older because of their Caucasian descent, but I was used to seeing that by now, so I was pretty good at estimating their ages. Unless they happened to be extraordinarily large or small compared to the average size, that is. And when determining someone's age, I also factored their environment into the equation. Orphans were often smaller than average because of their lack of nutrition. Fat orphans weren't really a thing, after all.

"...Orphans?" Reiko asked.

"Probably."

They were pretty much the textbook image of typical orphans. Their clothes had probably been decent at one point, but now they were looking a bit dingy. They weren't completely ragged or anything, but they probably would have been laundered if they were living in a normal household. Judging by the fact that their clothes hadn't been washed, it was safe to assume that they were orphans. Not only that, but these kids weren't even in a fit state for an orphanage.

...Come to think of it, this place used to be an orphanage, huh.

"Still, there are five- or six-year-old thieves and ten-year-old killers, so don't let your guard down!" I warned.

"I know!" Reiko nodded.

That was just how things were in this world, and it was the same in some countries on modern Earth. We were nothing but frail women who had grown up in a peaceful country. It was entirely possible that someone who had been desperately fighting for their life from an early age could take a moment's opportunity to stab us with a knife. There was no guarantee that we could use potions or magic in the split second that the blade was thrust at us, either.

Both Reiko and I occupied more of a back-line role, as long-range fighters. Besides, Reiko had never killed anyone before. I couldn't say with certainty that she would be able to do it when necessary. That's why we had to kill the enemy before they got too close. So...

"The intruders have reached the first line of defense. They are taking the main route..."

Huh, they were heading straight to the front entrance instead of trying to sneak in. They would have been greeted with trap holes and all sorts of surprises if they had gone around the side, but we obviously hadn't rigged up the main entrance like that. We may have had occasional visitors, after all, and we didn't want to accidentally trigger our own traps.

But considering the two were coming right up to the front, maybe they weren't here to steal anything. I figured the only time children would visit a stranger's house at night would be to steal or beg. And if they were beggars, they probably would have come by during the day or evening, when it was more likely that we would have leftovers. They definitely wouldn't have come so late at night.

I didn't want to reveal my secret unnecessarily, so I held a dagger in my left hand, with a bottle of explosive potion at my right hip. Reiko equipped herself with a short sword and a crossbow.

...Apparently, she had been training with all sorts of weapons in Japan to prepare for this day.

Damn it, I would've made preparations if I knew I was reincarnating, too!

In any case, we were fully geared up as we waited for the visitors to arrive.

Knock, knock!

Some time later, the knocker rang out. It seemed they really were just visitors, not burglars. But they were still two dirty-looking children arriving at such a late hour with no appointment. They definitely weren't what you'd consider proper guests.

Still, there was no point in pretending we weren't home. That would just be delaying the issue, and next time they might not try to come in through the front entrance. It was better to respond normally — no, with a friendly demeanor, so we could gain more information.

"Coming!"

So, I opened the door and greeted them cheerfully, and...

"Eek!!!"

The two kids fell back on their butts.

"D-Don't kill us!"

Oh.

I had a dagger in my left hand, and Reiko was behind me aiming a crossbow at them. I couldn't blame them for getting scared...

"...So, you two used to live here?"

"Y-Yes, I grew up in the orphanage here... I was taken in by a merchant in a neighboring territory, but I was put to work as a slave instead of cared for as a foster daughter as was originally promised... Then I started to feel like I was in danger, so I ran away as soon as I had the chance. He was just recently brought in from another orphanage, and I took him with me..."

Oh, that's heavy...

It sounded like whoever took them in intended to enslave them from the get-go... How evil.

"And you had nowhere else to go, so you came back here with a report on whoever took you guys in."

"Y-Yes..."

The girl had carried that younger boy all the way here, in a desperate attempt to escape with her life, and when she finally arrived, she was greeted by a dagger and crossbow instead of

179

the caretakers and the other children at the orphanage. No wonder she fell on her butt...

The nine-year-old girl, who was named Mine, desperately explained her story as the six-year-old Aral hungrily dug into his bread and soup.

I could have offered them some meat, but I heard that eating something that's hard to digest after eating nothing for a long time can make you puke, so I opted to give them some soft bread and soup instead. The soup was full of nutritious ingredients, though.

Mine also had some bread and soup before she started talking. She didn't eat much, so maybe she wasn't a big eater, or she knew that she wasn't supposed to stuff herself too quickly. But, seeing how she didn't try to stop Aral from eating, maybe she had a different reason.

Mine's real name was Minette, but she went by her shortened name in accordance with the rules at her orphanage. I found out that the kids at the orphanage were given short and easy-to-pronounce names, so the young kids could pronounce them, and so the caretakers could call them quickly to stop them from doing something dangerous.

If a child's name was known when they were taken in, they were often given a nickname if their name was too long or too difficult to say. Long names put you at a disadvantage when it comes to survival, anyway. There's even a Japanese cautionary tale about that called Jugemu...

Anyway, I decided to feed them and let them bathe and stay the night. Tomorrow, I'd ask the realtor where the owners of the orphanage had gone and then decide what to do about these kids. I'd feel pretty awful if they were to die on the streets or ended up in the slums just because I threw them out.

And most people may have seen them as "just orphans," but to me, they were just like Emile and the others from the Eyes of the Goddess. Pushing these kids away would be the same as pushing Emile, Belle, or Layette away. I had to at least find a place for them to stay before sending them off...

Come to think of it, this place had been an orphanage. Why had it ended up being sold as a vacant house? You didn't normally see orphanages go out of business. They weren't really commercial operations in the first place, so I doubted they'd had a downturn in revenue or that a rival company had driven them out of business...

Considering the country, lord, and people of the city all seemed fine, it seemed unlikely that an orphanage would get shut down so abruptly under normal circumstances. Maybe their operations had been funded by the national government, or possibly the local lord, or even donations from local residents, and their source of revenue had suddenly gotten cut off? Hmm, it was probably best to ask the realtor tomorrow...

I should have asked why this place had been sold off in the first place before I bought it. Maybe there had been some sort of an incident here, or it was one of those Oshima Teru properties...

Extra Story:
The Eyes of the Goddess's Desperate Battle

"Kaoru returned to her own world. I doubt she'll ever come here again. However, she might still visit this world, considering it belongs to her friend, Lady Celestine. But that could be several centuries or even millennia from now, and she might descend in another country or maybe even another continent. It would make more sense to visit places you've never been if you were going sightseeing, right?"

"…"

Emile made this rather callous statement to the six members of the Eyes of the Goddess and Layette. He really had no choice. They were going to find out eventually, and it was far better for them to hear the truth directly from Emile rather than through secondhand or embellished rumors. Lolotte was also there, having taken a day off from the workshop.

"Kaoru didn't leave of her own volition. I suspect she intended to stick around until we could all be independent… That's the kind of person she is, don't you agree?"

The other seven nodded. Indeed, Kaoru was that sort of person. Despite being a goddess, she was a strange deity, one who disliked being treated with reverence, and who wanted the orphans to address her casually.

The orphans had been troubled at first, but reluctantly did as they were told when Kaoru started addressing them with reverence and made everyone uncomfortable. They came to realize that it was truly isolating to be the only one being treated differently in the house, and they wanted to do as Kaoru wanted.

"Anyway, because of the unexpected damage to her temporary physical form, Kaoru had to go back to her own world earlier than planned, and her vacation here came to an end. Do you all realize what this means?"

The seven nodded.

"We all need to live on our own from now on, and we each have a responsibility. Anyone who sees us will think: 'Ah, so those are the orphans that Kaoru girl took care of.' If we were to ever do anything shameful…"

The other seven gulped hard.

"…Kaoru's name would be tarnished."

The children all grew pale. That couldn't happen. They would put their lives on the line to make sure that could *never* happen.

"Kaoru must have known this was a possibility. That's why she had us prepare, and why she taught us all sorts of things after returning from her trip. She must have been thinking about what would happen to us if she were to suddenly disappear… And we just poked fun at her and laughed it off…"

"But no one ever thought Big Sis Kaoru would actually get married…"

"Y-Yeah. Well, not much we could have done about that. I thought the same, and in the end, she left without ever getting married here…" Emile said in agreement to one of the orphans' comments.

They were quite harsh on Kaoru when it came to that subject…

"But putting that aside, the question is, what are we going to do from here? I mean, we won't have any issues getting by. Other than letting us live in her house, we've been doing fine without her financial support... Actually, we were the ones taking care of her, and we even have some savings."

Lolotte had been chipping in with her earnings from the workshop, and they had no rent, water bills, or electric bills to pay, and that left seven people's worth of income (excluding Layette). Their only expenses were food and firewood for cooking, and some occasional clothing purchases. Thrifted clothing, of course.

As for their income, these were kids who Kaoru was taking care of (or so people thought), so they had proper jobs. It went without saying that they would never get turned down if they applied for work somewhere. The children often turned down better opportunities, saying "I can't take care of Kaoru if I get home too late," or, "I can't work at places where I won't be able to gather intel for the Eyes of the Goddess." Still, they made decent money despite being selective about their work.

Of course, it wasn't that they got special treatment because Kaoru was taking care of them (or so people thought)... They could have gotten such special treatment if they wanted, but Kaoru and the orphans themselves would have never accepted that. The orphans' knowledge and thought processes were far above the level of other children in this world, thanks to Kaoru's teachings, making them each incredibly useful. They could greatly improve efficiency and profits with ease wherever they worked.

As such, there were no issues at all with how things stood currently. They could each work their way up at their places of work, get married, and continue building their careers or maybe even start their own businesses. That would let each of them lead a pretty decent life.

...The issue was, that wasn't what any of them desired.

"If we don't do something, Kaoru will be overshadowed by the Order of the Goddess! They claim that Lady Celestine is the one and only goddess, and they'll solidify Kaoru's position in history as a normal person with Lady Celestine's blessing. And…"

"We can't let that happen!!!" they all yelled.

"I talked to the Commerce Guild. They said that as long as we're just selling ingredients and not actual medicine, we won't need any apothecary-related licenses or permissions. We can register as a small, family-owned business that way."

"Good, it's just as I heard from Master Gruber, then. Let's rent out the house next door, under the condition that we can do construction work on part of the building, then ask a master carpenter to help us turn it into a storefront. Then we'll secure a supply route, and the older group will register as hunters to gather our own herbs. Then…"

Emile's gaze turned to a notice board nearby. It read, *Head Temple of the Goddess Kaoru.*

Indeed, the objective of the orphans was to carve Kaoru's name and achievements into history.

"We must establish an economic infrastructure so we don't have to rely on believers, donations, missionary work, or expansion. We'll create an organization that only serves to record facts and historical information to be passed down into the future. All so that one day, when Kaoru descends upon this world again, we can show her all the good that came of her actions, from how she had saved us all… Let's do this, guys!"

"Yeeeaaah!!!" they shouted in unison.

"I heard you started something interesting…"

"Why are you here, Fran…?"

"Let me have a bite!"

"You too, Roland?"

"What's this I hear about a religion giving praise to Lady Kaoru?"

"Who are you…? Oh, you're Carlos's owner… Your eyes are so similar to Kaoru's, you scared me for a sec…"

"We owe much to Lady Kaoru. If a new religion has been founded in her honor, we would not be opposed to converting…"

"Who are you guys…? Wait, what? Admirals of the Aligot Imperial Navy? And you're the chairman of the shipowners' association?"

"Things are getting real here…"

"Yeah. But I doubt we'll get any more people than this. We should be good as long as we have enough authority to repel anyone from Lady Celestine's order that tries to give us flak…

"All right, the Order of the Goddess Kaoru Head Temple is officially up and running!"

The orphans had suddenly started a new religion. The religion claimed that Saint Kaoru, a messenger of the Goddess who had saved orphans and prevented a war between nations by sacrificing herself, was a goddess herself. The religions of this world had split off into many sects, but it treated the Goddess Celestine as the one and only deity. In other words, worshiping any other god was seen as heresy.

…However, even believers of the Order of the Goddess Celestine couldn't take too strong of a stance against this new religion. Kaoru was the Angel of the Goddess Celestine, and was now praised as a saint after her passing. Plus, Kaoru had saved the lives of the orphans who had started the religion. In their eyes, she was indeed akin to a goddess. No one dared deny their beliefs or brand it as heresy. Priests, especially. That is, any priest who cared about their reputation among the people…

Not to mention, it was backed by the great hero and guardian of the continent, Fran, and the brother of the king, Roland, and their support wasn't just from aristocrats from their own country. A noble girl from another land who was known for being loved by the Goddess, members of the Aligot Imperial Navy, and owners and crews of merchant ships had put their full support behind the movement. Considering they had no intention of spreading their influence and showed no signs of ill intent, it was pointless to get burned going after such a small religious group.

Indeed, leaving them alone was the best option. They figured the best way to resolve this without making waves was to treat them as one of the many small sects that had splintered from the Order of Celestine…

And a few years later…

"We have a package from Beliscas!"

"Good. The merchant ships from the Aligot Empire will be entering the ports next week. The cargo being carried in the battleships should be arriving even sooner. I want the harvesting team to stop their work after today and give them some backup. I'll put in a request to the Hunter's Guild to take care of the harvesting instead."

"Roger that! Hehe, we're a 'family business,' so we don't have any overhead, the empire's navy accommodates us in exchange for giving them some alcohol, and the merchant ships take care of shipments for a small fee, so there's no way any merchant can compete with our prices. Maybe we can monopolize the supply routes of the royal capital's apothecaries…no, I guess we can't…"

"Haha, right..." The young boy came to his own conclusion without Emile having to say it.

Nothing good came from going too far with anything. What would happen if a business claimed the sole supply chain of an important resource, then suddenly went out of business? No matter how steady a business might be, a key product could suddenly become unavailable due to unfavorable weather, war, or some other unexpected reason. Moreover, a company that one was doing business with could suddenly shut down before they paid off their balance, or a thief could break in and steal the money or the products. Even worse, bandits could kill all of the workers and even set the shop on fire...

These might be bandits who just wanted to steal something, or those who were hired by someone. For example, by the owner of a large business or major shop who had their market share taken by an up-and-coming store that had undercut their prices... And if a business that monopolized the supply suddenly went bankrupt, distribution of that product would stop completely. This wouldn't be an issue if it was a non-essential or luxury item, but anything related to human lives was another story... And, of course, ingredients for medicine fell into that category.

...It was best to make "just enough" in business. Going too far would be asking for trouble.

"Well, we'll make some decent earnings with the ingredients for medicine. And if we ever stop making money, we can always change course..."

...Some time later, the house next to the orphans' house on the other side of the apothecary was purchased outright. Yes, they had already earned and saved enough for such a major acquisition. They had already purchased the apothecary several years ago, after all.

Business was going smoothly. This was no surprise. After all, they had powerful weapons in their arsenal:

Kaoru's name value.

A powerful sense of unity and familial love that far surpassed that of a real family...

And the knowledge and business tactics from Earth that Kaoru had ingrained into them.

No one could possibly compete...

"Huh, there's a new shop two buildings over from the apothecary. Let's see... 'The Eyes of the Goddess Souvenir Store'? That apothecary also had 'the Eyes of the Goddess' in it, and I think it's run by those former orphans..."

No one called Emile and the others of the Eyes of the Goddess "orphans" anymore.

These days, they were referred to as "former orphans," "the boys/girls from Kaoru's place," or "those Nagase boys/girls." The last one was because the children had given themselves the last name Nagase, and the townspeople assumed it was their shop name or something. The actual shop name was "The Eyes of the Goddess"... Besides, the former orphans were considered adults now that they were over fifteen, making them too old to be referred to as just "orphans."

And at the new store, there was a notice that read, "Get your Lady Kaoru rice crackers here!"...

"Rice crackers?"

Rice crackers, known as senbei in Japan, were already being made in the Jomon and Yayoi eras, but it seemed they either weren't being made here or weren't commonly known, judging from the man's unfamiliar tone.

"Guess I'll take a peek inside…"

There were various items featured in the shop.

The "Lady Kaoru Wooden Doll," the "Lady Kaoru Stuffed Doll," the "Lady Kaoru Mask," the "Lady Kaoru Evil-Warding Doll," "Lady Kaoru Rice Crackers," "Lady Kaoru Charms," *All About the Order of the Goddess Kaoru*," "*The Lady Kaoru Diet*"…

The harsh look in the eyes of the mask and evil-warding doll were extremely accurate to the source material, and were said to be very effective at keeping evil at bay. The two books, which could also be found in libraries, had been written by Emile and Belle, respectively. The diet method was indeed effective at losing weight, but it mainly reduced weight from one's breasts, making it not so popular.

Belle was quite upset at the complaints and shouted, "It *does* say it's the 'Lady Kaoru' Diet, doesn't it?!"

In any case, these products had been in stock for a long time, and were still being sold by the time Kaoru was resurrected. It was a good thing Kaoru happened to walk into the apothecary instead of the souvenir store…

"We're going to live. We'll have descendants, who will continue to protect Kaoru's legacy. Let's trust in the possibility that Kaoru will one day come to see it all with her own eyes…"

"Yeah!" they all yelled.

"…And for now, Belle and I have had our first descendant between us…"

"Teehee!"

"Tch!" the others said.

"Achille and I have a child as well…" said Lolotte.

A second, louder "Tch!" came even louder from the childless ones.

"We'll fulfill Kaoru's unrealized dream of living a happy married life…"

"If Big Sis Kaoru heard that, she would probably shout…"

"Sh-Shaddap!!!" they all cheered together.

Extra Story:
Mariel and the Three Vows of the Silver Breed

"Wha…"

I-It couldn't be… L-Lady Kaoru…passed away…?

No, that's impossible! The Goddess couldn't possibly have died!

She must have gotten tired of the folly of humans and returned to her own world. …But those who caused her to do so were absolutely execrable. Those pieces of garbage stamped out any possibility for me to ever reunite with Lady Kaoru in this world again… Unforgivable.

…They will pay!!!

Death to those fools! Their suffering will be worse than hell itself. They would spend their lives wallowing in regret.

…Hmhm.

Hmhmhmhm.

Hahahahaha…

"We are heading to the Kingdom of Brancott. Prepare to depart at once!"

"Whaaaaaaaaat?!" came a dozen voices all at once.

I shook off His Majesty and the other aristocrats as they desperately tried to stop me, then hopped onto Carlos and rode toward Aras, the capital of Brancott. The survivors of Rueda's demise could still be around, so it would be dangerous for a messenger of the Goddess to go, they said… Such nonsense, considering I was heading there to crush them in the first place…

Besides, Sir Ed, to whom I am greatly indebted, might not know what was going on. I had no intention of stopping at the whim of mere royalty or of the high-ranking nobles when he might need my help. I had to do what little I could to repay my debt. Not to mention, I had to seek out my prey to unleash this pent-up anger on them. It would take far too long by carriage. I would ride Carlos and take a handful of retainers and guards with me for this emergency trip.

…It's dangerous for a young noblewoman to go on a journey with such a small group, you say? Several dozen large dogs running alongside me and just as many birds of prey flying overhead accompanied me. No bandits were brave enough to attack a group surrounded by such an unusual entourage. Besides, the rumors of the "Bird Aristocrat," a messenger of the Goddess protected by dogs and birds, had become quite famous. Bandits of neighboring countries were sure to have heard of me by now… As well as what had happened to my enemies…

"Make haste, Carlos!"

"Breeheeheehee! (Yes, my lady!)"

"…We were too late…"

By the time we arrived at the royal capital of Aras, it was all over. The culprits had already been disposed of, and those who had fled had already been hunted down… There was no outlet for my rage left…

"Brehehe, brehehee… (My lady, we must get to Sir Ed…)"

Ah, that's right! I must get to him right away, in case he hasn't been informed of the situation!

"To the capital of Balmore!"

"Yes, my lady!" my attendants said at once.

"...I see, the little missy went home, huh..."

"I see you aren't too surprised..."

"Well, she's a Goddess, after all..."

Although he didn't seem too surprised, I could see the sorrow in Sir Ed's eyes. His wife and daughter were sad as well.

"I'm sure she didn't expect having to leave so suddenly. Not much that could be done about that... Guess we'll do what we can to prepare for the future... Anyway...farewell, Old Man Carlos! Oh, and little missy, would you mind stopping by again in a few years? I'd like you to translate for me and help apply a little pressure."

"Yes, of course! I could never hope to repay the debt I owe you. If you ever need me, I'll be there right away!"

"Appreciate it..."

A few years later...

I returned to the capital of Balmore, as Sir Ed had requested, and entered the ranch where he had been staying, which I later found out was also where his wife had been born. I stood between him and the ranch owner and arranged several promises between them.

Among them, there were several items that had been particularly emphasized by Sir Ed, which would later be known as the Three Vows of the Silver Breed, eventually thought to be a mere legend or folktale...

1: Sir Ed's descendants shall hereby all be known as Silver horses.

2: Silver horses shall have the right to choose their own owners. They could usually be sold or purchased as normal, but if they showed an unwillingness to go with a particular owner, they must not be sold, no matter the price offered. Conversely, if they showed a willingness to serve a particular owner, their will must be respected, and they must be given up at the appropriate market price.

3: If these stipulations are broken, the ranch will lose all rights of stewardship over the Silver horses, and all members of the Silver horses shall rise in opposition against the ranch. If this is to ever happen, House Raphael will take them in instead.

The ranch owner stared wide-eyed, but Sir Ed's resolve had been set, stating, "If you don't agree, I'll leave immediately. Even if you try to stop me, I won't sire any more offspring or obey your orders. I'll order all of my descendants not to listen to any orders from any humans, too."

The ranch owner reluctantly agreed. That said, Sir Ed did assure him that he wouldn't make use of these rights unless something drastic were to happen...

In any case, the Three Vows of the Silver Breed had been officially agreed upon, by the names of the ranch owner, Sir Ed, and our own House Raphael...

These conditions were also announced to the general public. This was to prevent any influential people from forcefully trying to own a Silver horse they liked. In the end, the stipulations of the agreement were never acted upon, and they were eventually thought to be a made-up story meant to keep the powerful in check, or to increase the perceived value of the Silver horses.

...But I still remember Sir Ed's happy smile from when the agreement had been made. That was a face of joy, a face of someone who knew they had accomplished something important. I'm certain he must have known. He knew that, one day, this agreement would be useful.

And there was only one moment I could think of that the Silver horses — Sir Ed's descendants — would ever need to act under such conditions. The day that glory would once again return to the Silvers. The day that Sir Ed's descendants would rise as divine horses... He truly believed from the bottom of his heart that the day would come, just as he had no doubt that she would choose his descendants as her cherished mounts when the time came.

It seemed that Emile and the others were making all sorts of preparations for that day. ...In that case, so should I. I would plant the seeds for that day to come, making the necessary preparations. Even if my life didn't last until that day, my children, grandchildren, great-grandchildren, great-great-grandchildren, or even their descendants would be there to serve her.

I believe...

But before that happened, perhaps I would be able to see her directly. Not in this world, but in the heavenly realm where Lady Celestine and Lady Kaoru reside...

Afterword

Hello again, this is FUNA.

It has been three years since volume 1 was released.

I Shall Survive Using Potions! has finally reached volume 6! We couldn't have done it without all of you readers. Thank you very much.

Please continue to support the series! Kaoru got carried away and went charging into the enemy ranks, then was easily defeated.

It seemed that those two were the ones who understood her best after all…

A reunion with an old friend, and a departure from her companions.

Is the trio of Kaoru, Kyoko, and Reiko (KKR) doomed to go out of control without Kyoko to keep them in check? Kaoru's office, Little Silver, will be open for business in the next volume! And a mysterious girl appears. But is she a friend or foe…?

Kaoru: "I'll keep working slow and steady with my cheat powers!"

Reiko: "Aren't you kind of contradicting yourself?!"

Where are Kaoru and Reiko off to with orphans again…?

Things may be tough with the coronavirus going around… We may be staying indoors, but because we're in times like these, let your heart run wild through stories!

To my editor, the illustrator Sukima, the binding designer, the proofreading supervisor, the publisher, distributor, bookstore workers, managers of the light novel publishing website Shosetsuka ni Naro, everyone who pointed out typos and gave advice and ideas in the comment section, and everyone who picked this book up, I am grateful from the bottom of my heart.

Thank you! I hope to see you again in the next volume...

FUNA

J-Novel Club Lineup

Ebook Releases Series List

* Novel and Manga Editions
** Manga Only

Keep an eye out at j-novel.club
    for further new title
    announcements!